# PIECES OF US

## MISSING PIECES SERIES, BOOK THREE

### N.R. WALKER

# COPYRIGHT

## BLURB

*Missing Pieces Series, Book Three*

As Justin's recovery moves forward, Dallas dares to hope their lives are settling into their new normal. His money worries have eased, business is picking up, and best of all, Justin now laughs more than he frowns.

Justin's memory still eludes him, but with each snippet or flashback, small pieces of his old life start to slot into place. He remembers more of Dallas and how perfectly happy their lives used to be, and with each passing day, Justin realises he can have that again.

But when someone from Justin's past turns up, he discovers that not all the missing pieces are good, and sadly, he and Dallas also learn just what it means to live with a traumatic brain injury.

If Dallas and Justin have to fight for their Happily Ever After, then Dallas will stop at nothing—*nothing*—to give Justin the life he always wanted.

---

"*. . . as I tried to put the puzzle of myself back together, it was the pieces of us that made me whole.*"

MISSING PIECES SERIES
BOOK THREE

# PIECES OF US

# CHAPTER ONE



I WAS UP BEFORE DALLAS, which was unusual, drinking my decaf coffee and staring out the kitchen window. He was normally awake before me, but a headache somewhere around five in the morning had me up searching for my pills. Headaches were nothing new; sometimes I'd catch myself thinking life was returning to normal, but then the constant pain inside my head reminded me otherwise.

I was so used to headaches now I barely registered them. That continuous ache was sometimes dull, sometimes sharp, but always there. Except for this morning when it woke me up.

I was never too cheerful in the morning, but today I was feeling particularly sorry for myself. Not even watching Dallas sleep improved my mood. If anything, it made me feel even shittier. He was so good to me. He was, without doubt, too good for me as well.

But for some stupid reason, he loved me. He loved me before the accident, and that didn't change anything for him. If anything, he reckoned it made him realise he loved me more now. It had been a lesson in taking things for granted, he'd said. I could see it in his eyes just how much he loved me. Those hazel-grey eyes couldn't hide a thing, and I found myself recognising his moods in them.

Losing myself in them.

Dallas had said that we fell in love hard and fast the first time, and it was much the same for me the second time. He was caring, attentive, thoughtful, funny . . . everything I ever wanted in a boyfriend. He was also tall, strong, and handsome. How on earth I'd ever scored him once was a mystery to me. The fact he'd stuck around for a second time was just crazy.

But stuck around he had.

I hated to think where I'd be without him. If I'd decided not to go home with him when we'd left the hospital—not that I had anywhere else to go—well, they would have found me somewhere, apparently. But my heart said to go with him, and now I knew why.

Because my heart knew him.

My heart loved him.

And on days when I felt like shit—not just physically, but emotionally as well—I just felt . . . useless.

Like a kid who needed babysitting. Who couldn't walk up or down stairs without supervision, who couldn't even have a shower in the house by himself. And being at work was like my first day as a sixteen-year-old apprentice. I knew it was all for my safety or whatever, but that just pissed me off. I wasn't a kid. I wasn't incompetent. I knew how to do this stuff. And some days my brain was slow as hell; but some days my mind was fine and it was my body that betrayed me.

I hated being like this.

I hated being so dependent on other people. I hated that Dallas had to look after me like I was a toddler and how

Sparra had to babysit me at work. I hated that I was aware of just how much I couldn't do, of how much I used to do and now couldn't.

We'd spent a few hours on Saturday at Jimmy and Nancy's house, and I was so wiped out, it put my arse on the couch for all of Sunday. I napped on and off all damn day. I tried to do a few things around the flat with Dallas but was no good at anything.

He'd simply kissed me with a smile and told me to rest while he pottered about getting everything done while I parked up in front of the damn TV like a simpleton.

I couldn't help but wonder how long he'd put up with it. How long would it take until he realised he could have any guy he wanted who didn't have a brain injury? That didn't have a fucked-up leg and who didn't speak slow?

I heard the bedroom door open and didn't even have to turn around. The sound of his feet got closer, then his huge warm hand slid up my back. "Hey," he murmured. "I woke up alone."

I sighed, now feeling even shittier than before. "Sorry. Headache woke me up and I didn't want to disturb you."

"Oh, you feel okay?" he asked, concerned. "Want me to get your pills?"

I turned then and offered a small smile. "I already took one, thanks."

He put his fingers to my chin and inspected my eyes. "Baby, what's wrong?"

I shrugged. "I feel . . ." I couldn't find the right word. And it wasn't aphasia. There were just too many words to choose from: awful, like shit, bad, low, worthless, horrible, useless . . . "Sad."

Frowning, Dallas took my empty coffee cup from me, put it on the sink, and pulled me into his arms. Into those huge, strong, and warm arms, holding me against his chest where I was safe and protected and completely enclosed. I could feel my worries dissipate, and the tension left my shoulders as I melted into him.

It was such a relief and so comforting, I could have cried.

I was stupid to think for one second that I could live without him. Well, not that I thought *I* could, but I had wondered why he didn't leave me. *I wouldn't survive this without him.*

He rubbed my back and took deep, calming breaths which I somehow unknowingly mimicked, making myself feel a little better.

"I'm sorry," I mumbled.

"You don't have to be sorry," he replied. His voice rumbled smoothly in his chest against my ear. He never moved to let go of me or even pull away. "Did you feel sad for any reason? Or just because."

"Just because." I sighed since that felt like such an easy way out. I needed to talk about this. I owed him that. "I just feel . . . I hate being useless and I hate how my brain doesn't work sometimes. I hate that you have to look after me, and I hate that I can't do everything. I just woke up feeling pretty low today."

He rubbed my back some more and kissed the side of my head. "I get that," he said, still hugging me. "And you're allowed to feel those things. I can tell you that you're not useless, but I don't want to make what you feel invalid. Because if you feel it, then it's real and we need to work on why you feel like that." He pulled back then and cupped my face. "But baby, you're the strongest guy I know. You're determined and capable, and you've accomplished more in the last two months than you realise. I know you must be frustrated with everything, and I don't blame you. But if you could just see how far you've come."

I frowned, because I certainly didn't feel like that.

"You're allowed to feel useless and frustrated. And angry and sad," Dallas added. "Thank you for telling me."

I sighed again, sagging against the kitchen counter. "I would be so lost without you," I mumbled.

He kissed my forehead and pressed me up against the cupboard and wrapped his strong arms around me again, squishing my face into his chest. "I'd be lost without you too," he replied. But then one arm was gone from around me as he reached over to the kettle and flicked it on. "I'd be lost without coffee too."

That made me smile, despite my mood. "You drink decaf now." Another change he'd made for me.

"Just because it's a bit different now doesn't mean I still don't need it," he replied. I was certain that was aimed at me and not all about coffee. Because I was a bit different now and he still needed me . . .

Then he shuffled me over so he could keep one arm around me while he reached for the cups. "You can let go of me," I suggested.

"Nope. I can do both. I can make two coffees and give good hugs."

I managed a chuckle. *How had he managed to make me laugh?* "Yes, you can."

He turned his head. "Ugh. The milk's in the fridge. Black coffee it is."

I pushed him away with a laugh. "Get the milk."

He quickly grabbed the milk and came straight back to his spot, which was pressed tight against me, pushing me against the cupboard with one arm around me. I gladly hugged him back, using the magic of his hugs to fix me for as long as I could.

"Coffees are done." He sipped his. "Now, shall I try for toast?"

I chuckled again. "Depends where the bread is."

He leaned and stretched. "Got it."

But the margarine was in the fridge so he had to let go of me, which gave me a chance to sip my fresh coffee. He made breakfast and we shared triangles of Vegemite toast, and by the time we'd showered and dressed for work, I was feeling better.

I should have stayed in bed and hugged him there rather than getting up and wallowing by myself. Dallas knew how to fix me, and I was stupid to pretend otherwise.

He stopped me at the door. "You sure you're feeling up to work today?" Dallas asked. "How's your headache?"

"It's okay. And yeah, I need to work today."

He grinned. "Good. Because I need you to work today. You're part of the team, Juss, and I need all hands on deck this morning."

And there he went, telling me how not useless I was without even trying. I was part of the team. He needed me. No matter how small a job I did, he needed me to do it. I gave him a nod and even managed a smile. "Okay."

With that beautiful smile, he led the way downstairs. He had me open the front roller door and unlock the front gates; then he wanted me to check the stock levels and see if anything needed to be reordered.

I knew what he was doing.

He was making me not useless.

Sneaky bastard.

By the time Davo and Sparra arrived, I was actually feeling pretty good about myself. They were both keen to use the new coffee machine, so that gave us some time to talk about our weekends until we were interrupted by our first clients of the day.

Sparra and I went to work on an old Yamaha while Davo serviced an ATV, and Dallas did some time in his office until another client dropped off a KTM. "Hey, Juss, I need you with me for this," he said.

It was gonna be a pretty big job. The rider had stacked it on the trails, and there was damage to the front forks, suspension, steering shaft, handlebars, and the front tyre would need replacing. The rider, the teen nephew of the owner, was okay, thankfully. But they'd learned an expensive lesson about going downhill on a loose surface using front brakes. Such a rookie mistake on an awesome bike.

And for a few hours, Dallas had me doing everything I could physically do. He let me take lead and he helped me when I needed it. He was proving a point—that I wasn't useless—and when we'd taken the front brake hose line clamp off and we were on opposite sides of the bike, I watched as he ratcheted a bolt undone, concentration and sweat on his brow. He caught me smiling at him. "What?" he asked quietly.

"I love you," I replied. I hadn't meant to say those words, not in the workshop, not so blasé. Davo and Sparra hadn't heard a thing, not that I cared. But holy shit, this man . . .

His smile became a grin, the ratchet in his hand forgotten. He seemed a little lost for words.

"I know what you're doing," I added. "Giving me jobs I can do, making me feel not useless."

He chuckled and put the tool down. "Just proving a point. Did it work?"

"Maybe."

"It totally worked."

I laughed but met his eyes. "You do these little things for me, to help me, without having to say a thing. Everything you do for me, you do because you love me, and it's like the saying 'actions speak louder than words.' I never really knew what that meant. But now I do."

His eyes softened. "Juss . . ."

"It's an amazing feeling knowing you're loved, so I wanted you to know too. I've said it before, but I wanted to say it again. I need you to know, Dall."

He walked around my side of the bike, took my face in his hands, and kissed me. It was all soft lips and scruffy beard and far too brief. He pulled back and put his forehead to mine. "I know you love me, Juss. But you can tell me as many times as you want."

"I love you," I whispered this time, and he closed his eyes and smiled as though he could just bathe in those words.

The shop phone rang right then, interrupting us, and Dallas stepped back and took the call. "Muller Mechanics."

Sparra came over, looking concerned. "You okay, Jusso?"

I smiled at him. "Yeah."

"Oh, I just looked over when I heard the phone and saw Dallas holding your face . . ." He smiled. "You two bein' all lovey-dovey again, huh?"

I snorted and watched Dallas as he stood with the phone to his ear. "He's kinda wonderful, isn't he?"

Sparra put his hand to his heart and squinted at me. "Personally, not my type. Great bloke, but I prefer 'em a whole lot prettier. And, well, female."

I laughed at that and Dallas turned to look at me, his face serious. "Justin's right here. I'll put him on." He held the phone out to me. "It's Angela from the workers' comp place."

Needing to sit for a bit to give my leg a break, I took the call in the breakroom. "Justin Keith speaking."

Angela replied, talking a mile a minute, and it took my brain a second to change gears. Apparently, she had filed all the appropriate paperwork and ticked every box that needed ticking, all the medical reports and doctors' findings had supported the claim, and the matter had been resolved.

"What does that mean?" I asked. "I don't . . . I can't follow, sorry. Dallas said the medical costs were covered. And the van."

"Yes, that's correct. But this is a separate matter. This is your personal claim, Justin. We talked about this a few weeks ago."

The truth was, I couldn't really remember. I knew the claims were going on, but I couldn't seem to get my brain to think about money or process what any of this meant. "Uh, my memory isn't too good, sorry. That time was blurry for me." And even now, my words were coming slower. I'd had a busy morning and I hadn't slept much and I'd woken up strung out, and it was starting to catch up with me. "I'm tired, sorry. My brain doesn't work right when I'm tired."

"That's okay, Justin. I won't keep you. I just wanted to let you know that the claim is now resolved and a payment figure has been awarded in your favour."

"Okay, that's good."

"Would you like to know how much it is, Mr Keith?"

"Uh, I probably should, shouldn't I?"

She was quiet for a moment. "The amount awarded to you, Mr Keith, is three hundred and eighty thousand dollars."

As she spoke some more about getting the paperwork

and signing off on everything, my mind began to turn in circles. That was a lot of money and I knew it was, but I couldn't quite get a grasp on it, and then Megan drove into the yard and it was all a bit too much.

"Are you still there, Mr Keith?"

"Yeah, but my homecare nurse is here. I have to go. Did you need to speak to Dallas again?"

She said yes, we'd need to organise a time for an appointment to sign off on everything, so I got to my feet and found Dallas speaking to Megan near the stairs to the flat.

"Hey, Dall. Angela needs to speak to you," I said, passing him the phone.

"Everything okay?" he whispered, holding the phone to his chest.

"Yeah 's fine. Just tired is all. Might need a nap after my torture session with Megan though."

Megan laughed but studied me. "You look tired, Justin. Your boss isn't working you too hard, is he?"

I looked at Dallas. "Nah. He's kinda dreamy though, isn't he?"

Dallas laughed and went back to the phone call, and Megan held out a walking cane. "I brought a present for you, Justin."

I stared at the cane. It was black and looked perfectly fine as far as canes went, but I didn't want it. "No thanks."

She smiled. "You'll like it better than the scooter."

Well, no, I wouldn't. "It doesn't have wheels. I like the scooter 'cause I can go fast."

She laughed and rolled her eyes and followed me up the stairs. There was something I really wanted to ask her, and I'd kept reminding myself all weekend to ask her when I saw her on Monday . . .

Oh, that's right.

I took a seat at the dining table and waited for Megan to do the same. "Can I ask you something?"

"Of course you can," Megan replied.

"Well, I've been thinking about it a lot. And with my leg and m'arm, and m'head too, I guess, being what they are." I shrugged. "But I was wondering what'd be the best position for me and Dallas to have sex?"

# CHAPTER TWO

## DALLAS

I WAS PRETTY sure Justin would be sleeping after his homecare appointment. He'd been getting tired before Megan arrived, and I worried a little that I'd given him too much work to do this morning. He hadn't slept well and he'd been all out of sorts, but there was no way I was letting him believe for one second that he was useless.

Useless.

That fucking word.

The last thing in the world he was, was useless.

When Megan was finished, I met her at the bottom of the stairs. "How is he?"

"He's fine," she replied with a smile. "He was just about asleep on the couch before we finished, so I'd say he's gonna sleep for a while. I left the walking cane hanging over the back of a dining chair. If it's missing, ask him where he's thrown it to."

That made me smile. "Sure. Uh, he was kinda depressed this morning. I dunno if that's the right word, but he was real down on himself."

"He mentioned it. Said you were very good at making him feel better without him realising."

"He saw straight through me."

She smiled but gave me a serious look. "He's recognising his moods and that's a good thing. He can tell when he's not in a good headspace and he knows to ask for help. Mood swings and depression are very common, and in all honesty, he's been more stable than most I've worked with. Just keep an eye on him, and if these episodes become more frequent or more severe, notify his primary doctor and we'll look at some options." She put a hand on my arm. "But he's doing great. He's kept up his physio exercises and he's getting his strength back. I think you can expect some frustration in the coming weeks by what he wants to do versus what his mobility allows, but as long as he doesn't overdo it, I think he'll be fine."

I nodded. "Yeah, of course."

She smiled and went on her way, and I went back to work on the KTM. I picked up the ratchet I'd been using and smiled when I remembered the reason I'd put it down. Juss had told me he loved me. Unprompted, unnecessary, and yet completely believable. He'd just looked at me—like he used to look at me, before the accident—and said those three words that made my heart soar.

I didn't care that I'd kissed him at work, where the guys or customers could see. I didn't give one single fuck anymore. If I wanted to touch him, kiss him, tell him I loved him, I would. I would never waste an opportunity ever again.

"Oh my gawd," Sparra droned. "Jusso had the same look on his face earlier. That *I'm so in love* look." He grinned. "In case you didn't know, Dallas, that guy's giddy as hell over you. Again."

Davo smiled beside him. "Not again. Still. He never stopped. His brain just needed some time to catch up, that's all."

I couldn't help it. I was grinning at both of them. "Ah, yeah. He's . . . he's . . ."

"If you say he's kinda dreamy, I get to knock off early," Sparra said. "That's the rules."

I snorted. "What?"

"That's what Jusso said about you this morning. *He's so dreamy*," Sparra added, imitating Justin's voice. "Asked me if I agreed. Now, boss, I reckon you're a lot of things, but dreamy ain't one of 'em."

I laughed at that but couldn't help but ask. "Did he really say that?"

They rolled their eyes in sync, and Sparra laughed. "Thank God it's lunchtime," Davo said, walking into the breakroom. Sparra followed him and I put the ratchet back down and went in too. "Did you guys watch the footy last night?" Davo asked.

"Nope," Sparra said proudly. "I had a date."

Davo and I stopped and stared. "A date?"

Sparra grinned. "Yep. Wasn't gonna say anything. But this is the third weekend in a row I've seen her, so maybe it might be something."

Sparra told us all about Carissa, how they'd met, and how he'd asked her out for dinner, and it was really good to sit and listen to him. He was excited about the prospect of a girlfriend, though he was trying not to read too much into it just yet. They were seeing each other again on Wednesday night. That sounded pretty promising to me. He showed us a selfie of them on his phone, and she looked sweet and he looked happy.

I loved hearing about someone else's life for a while, as

weird as that sounded. I'd been so absorbed in our lives, I'd lost touch of where they were up to.

"You might get to meet her this weekend," Sparra said. Then he gave me an uncertain look. "If we're still gonna meet up at the pub for lunch and the footy?"

Oh, I'd forgotten about that.

And you know what? Sitting around talking shit and having a laugh for a few hours sounded exactly like what I needed. "Absolutely. Not sure how long we'll be there for. We went out for a few hours on Saturday and it knocked Juss around a bit. He was pretty wiped yesterday. So I'll see what he says, if he thinks he's up for it. But I'm not gonna lie, it sounds damn good to me."

Then I remembered something else. "Oh, that reminds me. Justin and I have some appointments tomorrow: one at nine, then another one at ten. We shouldn't be too long. Doctor's appointment first, then we just need to sign some papers or something and we'll be straight back. We've only got two jobs in tomorrow and I was gonna spend most of the day in the office anyway."

Talk turned to work and what else we had booked in this week, and then we each went back to the bikes we were working on. I got busy and lost track of time and by three o'clock, I still hadn't heard anything from Juss, so I went upstairs to check on him.

The couch was vacant, though the TV was still going. The walking cane still hung over the chair. "Juss?"

"In here."

I followed the sound. The bathroom was empty, and I found him sitting on the edge of my side of the bed with a confused look on his face.

I walked in. "Everything okay?"

He met my eyes. "Oh yeah. I'm just looking for something. I think."

That didn't sound good. "Anything I can help you with?" He made a face, and was that a blush? I sat beside him on the bed. "Juss, what is it?"

He swallowed hard, suddenly nervous. "Oh God, I don't know how to say this . . ."

"Say what?"

"Well, I've been thinking. A lot. About . . . Ugh, about sex." He glanced at me, then looked back at his hands. "And I asked Megan today about stuff and she mentioned a few things that I haven't even thought about. And I should have. It was stupid of me not to. I mean, I trust you, and you didn't bring it up either. Not that we've really talked about it."

"Juss, baby. What are you talking about?"

He reached over and opened the top drawer of the bedside table. "I found lube," he said, his cheeks red. "But no condoms. I can't find them anywhere. I assumed we used them, because I've never not used them. Did we just run out? Or did you throw them out? I looked in the bathroom and in our wardrobe. Because if we're working on maybe having sex one day, we should have them."

Oh Christ.

Was he ready for this? Was I ready?

I took his hand. "Juss, we haven't used condoms for a long time."

He stared at me. Like, stared.

"We did, in the beginning, of course," I added. "But we agreed to be monogamous and faithful, and baby, I haven't even looked at another guy. Not once, not ever. So we got tested and we stopped using them."

"We . . ."

I nodded. "Yes. We used to have sex without condoms."

"That means . . ." He blushed, hard, his eyes wide. Then he whispered, "You'd come inside me."

Fuck.

My blood got a whole lot warmer. I nodded.

He licked his lips and swallowed hard, and it took a moment for him to look at me. "That's really fucking hot."

I barked out a laugh. "Uh, yeah. Every time."

He let out a long breath. "Damn."

"And you know what?" I said. "You're right. I should have brought this up with you before now. It was kind of irresponsible of me not to. But I didn't want to talk about sex in case you felt I was pressuring you. The last thing you need is for me to keep talking about it. But we should absolutely go and be tested again."

"No, we don't have to," he said, shaking his head.

"Yeah, we should. This is all new to you. Everything is new, so you should absolutely know, without any doubt, that we're being safe."

"I do trust you," he whispered.

"I know, baby. But for our own peace of mind." I kissed his knuckles. "If we get to do everything over again for a second-first time, then we should do *every*thing."

Justin chuckled and put his free hand to his forehead. "Okay."

"We can go tomorrow. The clinic is super quick, from memory. Or we could ask Doctor Chang in the morning and get a pathology request form."

He made a face. "Clinic's fine."

"We have an appointment to sign off on the workers' comp papers after we see Doctor Chang," I said. "We can go after that, if you're not too tired."

Juss nodded and gave me a smile. "I can't believe I was worried to talk to you about this."

"You don't need to worry. You can ask me anything."

"I can't believe we . . . go bareback." The blush flared on his cheeks. "Was it . . . I mean, is it . . . ?"

"The hottest sex ever? Yes. Is it the most beautiful kind of lovemaking?" I nodded. "Yeah. Well, it was for us. I never felt closer to you than I did when we did that."

He let out a shaky breath and met my eyes. "I want our first time—I mean, our second-first time—when we have sex, I want it to be like that."

I kissed him. "When you're ready, Juss. I'll make it so good for you."

# CHAPTER THREE

JUSTIN CAME BACK DOWNSTAIRS with me, but he mostly stuck to light duties. He helped me finish off the KTM but then unhurriedly tidied up for Davo and Sparra. He seemed content to go slow, just at his pace, and I was more than happy to encourage that.

It was . . . peaceful.

When the guys left, we locked up and Juss finished sweeping out while I sorted out some bookings and which parts we needed to order in. Finishing before me, he leaned against the doorframe to my office. "Hey."

I smiled up at him. "Hey. You done?"

He gave a nod. "What did you want for dinner?"

"There's minced beef in the fridge."

"It's gotten cold out," he murmured. "So maybe something . . . like meatloaf and mashed potato."

"That sounds great."

"I wasn't gonna make it. I was suggesting it."

I barked out a laugh. "Is that right?"

He smiled. "I guess I could help."

I shut down my laptop and stood up, and when I

walked to him, he didn't move. I expected him to step out of the doorway or move so I could walk through, but he didn't. He looked up at me with something in his eyes I hadn't seen in a long time.

Fire.

He leaned his back against the jamb, his eyes on mine, and he waited . . .

It was an invitation I had no intention of refusing.

I pressed against him and captured his mouth with mine. He responded in kind, kissing me with equal passion. He pulled me closer, our bodies aligned that perfect way they always did. He was turned on, hard already, and feeling his erection pressing against me made me groan into the kiss.

He slid his hand down over my arse, and that was . . . new. I mean, not for the old Justin. He'd done that a million times, but this new Justin hadn't really been inclined to explore too much.

And then he squeezed.

I broke the kiss with a laugh. "Hello there," I said, pulling his bottom lip between mine. We needed to cool it a little.

"I think we should go upstairs," he whispered.

Or we could not cool it at all.

I hit the lights, locked the door, and took Justin's hand. He could have easily walked up those stairs, but we got to the bottom and he slung his arm over my shoulder. "Carry me."

Grinning, I picked him up bridal style and carried him up. He never took his eyes off my face, the heat of his gaze burning into me. Once inside, I gently put his feet to the floor next to the couch. But he didn't pull his arm away. Instead, he trailed his hand along my neck and down my chest where he fisted my work shirt and pulled me toward him.

I walked him backwards until his arse hit the back of the sofa, and with a hand to my jaw, he pulled me in for a hard kiss.

He was so into it. Like a switch had flipped in his head, like some part of his brain had woken up.

This was just like the old Justin.

Justin, before the accident, was all about sex. He loved it. He was horny all the time, wanted me to suck and fuck him almost every damn day. I wasn't kidding when I told him we had a lot of sex. But I also wasn't kidding when I told him I'd wait until he was ready.

He'd been pushing boundaries in the last week or so, but this was . . . this was quite a step. And it was freaking hot.

My dick was definitely into it, and the hardness of Juss' erection felt divine.

I kissed him deep, tangling our tongues and sucking on his bottom lip, while grinding my hips into his. I was trying to be mindful of his leg, but the way he gripped me and grinded, I assumed his leg was feeling okay.

I slipped my hand between us and palmed his erection. "Tell me what you want, Juss," I murmured against his mouth.

"I want . . . I want your mouth . . . on me. Right here."

Oh, hell yes.

I dropped to my knees, sliding down his body, my eyes locked on his. I undid the button and fly of his work pants and let them hang open, off his hips. I nudged his cock with my nose and inhaled the scent of him before I pulled his briefs down and freed my prize.

He was leaning against the back of the couch, his legs

spread comfortably with me between his feet. The last thing I wanted him to do was strain his leg or his arm ... I wanted him to feel nothing but pleasure.

I licked the underside of his shaft, from his balls to the tip, and he groaned, frustrated, and he shook his head. He clearly didn't want me to tease him or drag this out, so I licked the head and tasted his slit before taking him into my mouth.

"Oh, fuck yes," he said.

I worked him over, swirled my tongue, sucked on the head, and pumped his base. He began to thrust his hips. This was what he wanted. This was what he needed.

I took him all the way in and looked up at him. He was staring down at me, his eyes dark, his lips open. He put his fingers through my hair. Then he touched my face and he drew his thumb along the side of my mouth, feeling how my lips surrounded his cock.

So I swallowed around him, and it pushed him over the edge. He cried out and his body flexed tight as he came down my throat.

He tasted like heaven.

When he was done, I got to my feet to make sure he was okay. "How're you feeling?"

He replied by laughing and taking my shirt and pulling me in for a hug. A few aftershocks tremored through him but he just chuckled. "Fucking hell."

I kissed his forehead, his eyelid, his nose, but when I went to take a step back, he had hold of my shirt and didn't let go. His eyes took a second to focus. "Your turn."

"Juss, you don't have to."

"I want to," he replied firmly. "Please, can I?"

Fucking hell. As if he'd ever have to beg. I looked around to where might be the best spot—he certainly couldn't kneel on the floor—but Juss took my arm and pulled me toward the coffee table. He sat on it, his right leg out straight, and grinned up at me.

"This is a good height," he said.

I laughed and he tugged me closer. Fuck. He pulled open my work pants, rough and eager, and then delicately took out my cock like he was about to defuse a bomb.

"Oh fuck," he breathed. "It's so beautiful." He studied every detail, every angle, and I had to remind myself that this was new to him. He was probably committing everything to memory. He lifted it and gave me a long stroke. "It's huge, Dallas. Like a porn star."

I scoffed and was about to reply when he flattened his tongue and sucked on the head of my dick.

*Oh fuck.*

"I've thought about this," he murmured between licking and sucking. "A lot."

"Have you?" I was panting, not sure what else to say. I was so hard, it was almost painful.

"Since you told me we don't use condoms." He looked up at me as he sucked me like a lollipop. "I've been imagining how it feels."

Christ, I was gonna come so fast.

He explored with his hands, touching, feeling, pumping, sliding with his tongue . . .

"Baby, I'm gonna come."

He smiled as he took me into his mouth, deep and wet heat. I gripped the back of his head and he groaned, and that was all it took. I filled his mouth and he hummed between swallows.

Fuck.

He released me and I swayed, my blood was buzzing,

my bones were like jelly, and he held my hips. "You okay there?"

I put my hands under his arms and lifted him to his feet so I could hold him. Or so he could hold me. I wasn't sure which. I just needed the contact.

I needed him.

"You okay, babe?" he whispered.

I nodded into his neck. "So very okay."

He chuckled. "Just so you know, I asked Megan which positions we could try that won't hurt my leg."

I snorted and pulled back. "You did?"

"Yeah, I think she almost died."

I laughed and kissed him softly. "We'll figure it out, baby."

He sighed and met my eyes. "I don't think I'm scared anymore. I don't even know why I was. I just couldn't bear the thought of pain or being vulnerable, I dunno why. I know you won't hurt me."

"I wouldn't."

"I used to love sex."

I smiled. The truth was, he loved it *a lot*. "You did."

"And I think about how gentle you are and how kind you are and how you know what I need," he whispered. "And I began to imagine what that would be like in bed. What you'd be like, how you'd treat me, and what you'd do to me. And my body was like, 'hell yes,' and my brain was like, 'okay, even I agree to that.'"

I laughed. "Glad they agreed."

"They haven't agreed on much since the accident," he replied dryly. "But they agree on this. Mostly my body, not gonna lie. But Dallas, I want it. I want you. I've had enough pain in the last few months to last me a lifetime. I want to feel good. I want to know what pleasure is. And I know you'll show me."

"I will."

"Just promise me something . . ."

I cupped his face. "Anything."

"Please don't be mad if I freak out or need you to stop."

"Oh, baby. I would never be mad."

"Because your dick is huge."

I snorted out a laugh. "It's not really."

"Did it . . . did we ever have any . . . fitting issues?"

I laughed at that. "Ah, no." I traced his eyebrow with my thumb, down his jaw, and across his bottom lip. "Baby, you loved it. You'd beg for it. You wanted it for hours."

His nostrils flared and he swallowed hard. "Oh."

I kissed him softly and whispered against his lips. "I will make it so good for you, you'll never want it to end."

His dick twitched against mine. "Uh, maybe we can have toast for dinner. I think we need to go to bed," he said. Then he made a face. "I'm not ready for a sex marathon, but I'm sure you can make me come again. Maybe twice."

I kissed him deeper, giving him some tongue, and his dick pulsed again between us. "Toast for dinner it is."

***

WE BOTH SLEPT like the dead. I'd wrung two more orgasms out of him like he'd asked, but maybe the last one had been too much. His body couldn't handle that kind of muscle-expenditure, being so tense and taut, and as much as I'd tried to relax him, orgasms were a strain on a tired body.

But I'd had him lie on the bed, face down, his legs spread. I'd massaged and rubbed him down, sensually and intimately. Then with a little bit of lube, I'd rubbed his hole and fingered him, working him into a frenzy before I rolled him over and sucked him.

Then I'd knelt between his thighs and jerked off, spilling my come onto his belly. He was too tired to shower, so I cleaned him up and finally crawled into bed beside him. He wrapped himself around me and I held him just as tight.

"When we get the test results back," he'd mumbled. "I'll be so ready."

We fell asleep and I don't think either of us moved all night.

I was up before him and had the scrambled eggs on toast and coffees made as he came out of the bedroom. "Perfect timing," I said.

He scowled, which was completely normal for Justin first thing, but he was limping more than usual.

"You okay?" I asked.

"Sore."

"Oh, baby. I'm sorry," I said, helping him to his seat.

He sipped his coffee first. "Nah, 's okay. It's a good sore. Well, not *good*. Physio sore is a bad sore. Overdoing it sore is a bad sore. Sore from too much sex is good sore." He shrugged. "You know what I mean."

I couldn't help but smile a little. "I do. What I think was, coming three times last night was probably one time too many."

He picked up his fork. "Speak for yourself."

I snorted. "Okay, well, last night it was fine. Today, not so much."

"I'll be okay after a hot shower." He ate some breakfast and nodded. "This is good. Thank you. One day I'll cook you breakfast."

I stabbed some egg with my fork. "Juss, you've never been a morning person. Ever."

He made a face that was almost a smile. "Mornings'd be all right . . . if they started around lunchtime."

I laughed. "Good to know some things never change, though, right?"

He conceded a nod, then sipped his coffee. "You know, this decaf stuff just isn't great. Do you reckon I could have some real coffee one day?"

"We can ask Doctor Chang."

"We see her first, right?"

"Sure do. Nine o'clock." I checked the time on the microwave. It was six forty now. Plenty of time. "But today's gonna be pretty busy, Juss. We've got Doctor Chang first, then the meeting with Angela to sign off on all the van and the medical costs, and if you still wanted, go to the clinic after that. But we can see how you're feeling, and if it's too much, we can go to the clinic another day."

Juss bit into some toast. "I'll be fine."

"We can bring the scooter or the walking cane today."

He shot me a not-pleased look. "No thanks. I can walk to a few appointments. And anyway, pretty sure I'll be planted on the couch for the rest of the day. I was gonna spend the afternoon watching porn."

I almost choked on my eggs, and one of Justin's rare morning smiles formed behind his coffee cup. "I'm assuming Pornhub is still a thing? I haven't checked," he said.

After I'd collected myself and managed a mouthful of coffee, I gave a nod. "Ah, yeah."

"You know," he added, "for a long time, I didn't think about sex at all. Now I know it's a thing, I think about it a lot."

My dick was particularly interested in this conversation.

It was pressing awkwardly in my briefs and I had to shift in my seat. "That's a good sign, right?"

"I think so." He pushed his empty plate away and smiled at me. "Now, about that hot shower."

Fucking hell. "If I join you in there, we'll be late."

He stood up, and sure enough, his boxers were tented at the front. He made no attempt to hide it. In fact, he stood there and smiled when I couldn't take my eyes off it. "Pretty sure the doc said I wasn't to shower alone."

I laughed out a groan. This was the old Justin. This was the bossy, playful Justin that I'd missed like crazy.

He turned and made his way to the bathroom. I dumped all the plates in the sink and was naked before I got to the bathroom door. He laughed as I joined him in the shower, though he wasn't laughing for long.

I made short work of him, and me, then quickly ran the soap over both of us. He was still in an orgasm haze when I shut the water off and handed him a towel. "Did we get any work done?" he asked as he dried himself. "Before, I mean. When we first got together. Did we ever have days when we couldn't be stuffed going to work and just spent the day in bed? Because I feel like that's something I would have done with you."

I chuckled. "Not really. There were days we were late to open the shop and some weekends when we never bothered with clothes. But we never missed work, no."

He sighed. "Did we ever have sex on your work desk?"

I laughed at that. "Nope."

"The table in the lunch-break room?"

I grimaced. "Ew, no."

He smiled. "Yeah, I agree. But your desk . . ."

I tied my towel off around my waist. "We're not doing that."

He towel-dried his hair and grinned at me. "What about on the bike hoist? I reckon I could lie on that and press the button till I was the perfect height for you to . . . you know, give me a grease and oil change."

I laughed, like really laughed, but shook my head. "No. We didn't do that." I nodded to the door. "Come on. We need to get dressed."

We opened the shop up and got everything ready for Davo and Sparra, and we left not long after they'd arrived. Juss was still in a good mood and it easily rubbed off on me. Seeing him happy and positive filled me with a real sense of hope.

Doctor Chang seemed to pick up on it too. "How is my favourite patient?" she asked, smiling as we walked in. "You look happy, Justin."

"Yeah, I'm pretty good today." He told her about his shit day the other day, and how hearing the song "When The War Is Over" had brought back the memory of the accident because it was playing on the radio when the truck had hit him, and the pain that went with it.

Doctor Chang explained to him what she'd said to me over the phone and how, while it might have felt frightening and overwhelming, it wasn't uncommon. But Justin could only shrug.

"I kinda felt okay afterward. Not about the pain, but remembering the accident," he said. "It's probably weird, but I like that I can remember it. The unknown was always the scariest part. There was so much unknown. Still is, of the last five years, I guess. But I prefer to remember it, even if it's not a happy memory."

"That's not weird at all, Justin," Doctor Chang replied.

Then he told her about the good days he'd had this week and how he'd been out to lunch and what he'd been doing at work. He still needed to rest every day, but that was getting less frequent over time, and he could do more things and his mind was clearer. No, he hadn't remembered anything else this week, but he told her how he wanted to focus more on the now, not a past he couldn't really remember.

She smiled like a proud mum. "And Dallas," she pressed. "Seems like a positive week?"

"Yeah," I agreed. "There's been some changes. Good changes," I said to Justin with a squeeze of his hand. I looked back to the doc. "The other night, Justin was talking about the future, and that was . . . that was amazing. Just a few weeks ago, he couldn't think far enough ahead to know if he wanted lunch; now he's making plans, so it's a huge step forward. His mind fog seems to be really clearing now."

Doctor Chang nodded, and she spoke about cognitive improvements and recognising milestones and achievements, remediation and compensation. But no, she couldn't recommend he drink proper coffee because of how caffeine reacted with a TBI, but yes, exploring sexual intercourse was fine, and no, it was still too early to tell if he'd recover any more memories.

"So, Justin," she said. "I want to see you next week, and the week after that you're scheduled for a follow-up MRI and CT scans. Then if everything is as it should be and moving forward, we might see how you feel about follow-up appointments every two weeks instead of every week."

"Oh. If you think I'm ready for that."

"I do. I think you're ready to move onto the next phase of your recovery," she said. "These next scans will be the three-month mark. Then fortnightly appointments will take us up to the six-month mark. That's a big milestone. Then you'll move to monthly appointments until your next scans at the one-year mark." She smiled. "So we might still only be taking things one step at a time, but you're making some pretty big strides, Justin."

He looked to me and smiled before he squeezed my hand. "Sounds good to me."

We left Doctor Chang's office and Justin was still smiling. He was a little tired but he wasn't falling asleep on me like he used to when we left these appointments. "How you feeling, baby?" I asked as we drove out of the car park.

"I feel good. Bit pissed off that I can't have caffeine."

"One day." I chuckled.

"And I'm thinking maybe that stupid cane might not have been such a terrible idea."

"Is your leg sore?"

"Nah, it's just draining. I don't wanna trip over because I can't lift my feet. Don't tell Megan I said that."

I chuckled. "Doctor Chang seems happy with your progress."

He smiled. "I really like her, but I won't be sad to see her every second week instead."

I reached over and took his hand. "Me too, baby."

"Do you think we could get a coffee after this next meeting? I mean, just a shitty decaf one."

I laughed. "Sure, we can."

A short time later, we arrived for our meeting with Angela, and thankfully we didn't have to wait long. After some small talk, we sat in her office as she began to go through the files in front of her, and she explained to me, the way lawyers do, the itemised accounts for the van and the tools and then the hours and wages for Justin. It was everything she'd already told me and it was fair, so I was more than happy to sign off on it.

I couldn't sign it quick enough.

Next was Justin's lump-sum compensation. I knew he'd

be entitled to something, and his medical costs were now covered. Angela explained things to Justin, though I had to wonder how much he was taking in. He was doing a fair amount of nodding and smiling, but it was more out of courtesy than agreeing. I followed along, and again, she reassured us it was all procedure and, in her opinion, very fair.

"Not many others are so lucky. Though each case is assessed on its merits, yours is quite deserving," she said. "The funds will take some time to land in your account, because it's quite a substantial sum. But once this is lodged, it should be straight forward. No long wait like last time."

Justin nodded. "And we pay the medical bills with this, right?"

She shook her head. "No, this is separate. All the hospital bills are taken care of. This is your money." She glanced at me before smiling back at Juss. "To spend however you see fit. The sum of three hundred and eighty thousand is compensation for your accident."

Juss shrugged. "Oh, okay."

Three hundred and eighty thousand . . .

"I'm sorry, what?" I asked. "Three hundred and eighty thousand . . . dollars?"

Angela looked at me. "Yes. Did he not tell you?"

I shook my head, and Justin shrugged again. "I was going to," he said. "But then I had my appointment with my nurse, then I fell asleep, and then we talked about sex and I haven't been able to think about much else, sorry."

My mind was spinning, but not enough to realise he just talked about sex in front of Angela. She was blushing and somewhat horrified, and I couldn't help but laugh. "Sorry," I said to her. "We got sidetracked yesterday. I'm just a little stunned. That is quite a chunk of money."

Angela nodded. "I was happy with the result. The

doctors agreed there was a significant change to the quality of life and that there will be long-term effects for Justin, so it was awarded accordingly." She handed Justin the pen. "Are you ready to sign off on it?"

"I just want it all to be over," Juss said. "Actually, what I want is my memories back and to be able to drink coffee again. And to have a leg and a brain that work properly would be good, but I'll settle for this to be over so we can have some kind of normal again."

Angela smiled. "That sounds good."

Justin signed, though his signature wasn't great, and he smiled at me when he put the pen down. Angela talked for a bit more, handed us our copies of files, and told us she'd be in touch once the payments came through.

We walked back to my ute, slower for Justin's pace. He was getting tired now. But as soon as we were in, I burst out laughing. "You didn't tell me how much they said you were getting."

He just smiled and shrugged. "I forgot, sorry."

I shook my head, still disbelieving. "Juss, this sets you up."

He stared at me. "Me? Sets me up for what?"

"For life. For whatever you want."

He didn't smile. In fact, he stared out the windscreen and frowned. "What I want is my life back. What I want is for this to never have happened. I want to remember everything, and I want my head not to hurt. That's what I want. No amount of money can do that."

Shit.

"Oh, Juss, I'm sorry. That's not what I meant. Sorry, it's just a bit of a shock, that's all. I know the money doesn't make up for anything. That's not what I meant."

"I know." He sighed. "I don't mean to sound pissy. But I

don't want the money. And that's not fair because you've been stressed about money, but I haven't even thought about it all this time. I try to, and you've shown me my bank statements, but . . ." He shrugged. "I dunno. I guess I'll need to start."

I reached over and took his hand. "Baby, don't worry about it. We can have the bank set up a separate account for it that only you can access." Not that anyone could access his everyday account either, but I wanted him to know I wasn't including myself in this. "Just let it sit there earning you some interest until you're ready to look at it."

He met my eyes and managed a small smile and a nod. "Sounds good."

"You don't need to worry about it until you want to. Not anyone else."

"Thank you," he sighed. "It's just a bit overwhelming, I guess. But you always know what to do."

"Not always."

"To me you do. You're like some pillar of strength. When I don't know what to do, I know you'll help me."

His words got me right in the heart. I lifted his hand to my lips and kissed his knuckles. "Because I love you, Justin Keith. Always have . . ."

He smiled, tired and cute as hell. "Always will."

# CHAPTER FOUR

WHEN WE GOT to the health clinic, I asked Justin twice if he was still okay to go inside or if he wanted to leave it for another day, but he was adamant. He was tired, physically, but also mentally—a doctor appointment followed directly by a legal appointment was enough for anyone.

But Justin was determined.

He wanted to get this done.

And it didn't take long. The whole process was quick and easy.

"Do they really just send the results to your phone these days?" he asked as we were done and finally heading home. "The same day?"

"Yep. Some tests take longer, and if anything's positive, they usually ask you to make an appointment. But with the rapid testing, if you get the all-clear, it's just a text later that day."

"Jesus. It used to take two weeks."

I chuckled. "Some still do, but a lot's changed in five years."

He leaned his head on the headrest, looked at me, and

smiled. I was pretty sure I'd be carrying him up the stairs. He could barely keep his eyes open. "The guy swabbed my dick," he mumbled.

I laughed. "Yep." It was a full sexual health check. Swabs and bloods.

"You went before me, so I asked him if he'd ever seen a dick as big as yours."

I shot him a look. "You didn't."

He grinned sleepily. "Did. But he didn't answer me. Did smile though."

"Oh God."

He chuckled. "Tell me, what was my reaction when I saw your dick the first time?"

Jesus H Christ. So apparently when I said he could ask me anything, my dick would be a constant topic of conversation . . .

"Uh, well," I began. "You were . . . happy."

"Bet I was."

"You wanted it a lot."

His eyes were dreamy, tired; his smile was smug. "Bet I did."

I chuckled at the memory. "Actually, after the first time we had sex, we were in bed, up to about round three, I think it was, and you said my dick was better than when you got a Transformer truck for your birthday when you were six."

He laughed, a deep rumbling sound. "Oh my God. Optimus Prime. Loved that truck."

The sound of his genuine belly laugh made me laugh too. "You said it was just like a normal toy truck, then in bed it transformed, and *bam!* Optimus Prime."

Juss laughed again, but his eyes were closed. "Optimus Prime dick," he mumbled. Then he chuckled some more, even as he slept.

God, I'd forgotten about that whole Transformer conversation. When we first got together and he shoved his hands down my pants, he was like a kid in a candy store. And when we'd first fallen into bed together, he'd been insatiable.

I'd taken for granted all those memories. I never recalled them, never relished them, never thought for one moment I wouldn't miss them should they be taken away.

And there was Justin, who would give anything to have any of his memories back.

It was a sobering realisation.

***

I GOT some drive-thru lunch for all of us, pulled the ute into the workshop, and drove around the back near the stairs. Justin was sound asleep in the passenger seat. "Hey, Jussy. We're home."

He stirred when I opened his door, and when I leaned in to undo his seatbelt, he opened his eyes slowly and smiled. "Hey, you," he whispered.

"Hey, handsome," I said, giving him a quick kiss. "We gotta get you up these stairs. Then you can sleep."

He groaned and carefully lifted his right leg to set his feet on the ground. Sparra walked out, grinning. "How's the man of the moment?"

"The what?" I asked.

"Newspaper guy was here earlier. Wants an interview," he replied. "Said he'd call back tomorrow."

"An interview?" Juss asked. "Me? What for?"

Sparra shrugged. "The crash was pretty big news. He wanted a follow-up."

I resisted snarling, but Justin just snorted. "Must be

hard up for news," he mumbled as he made his way to the stairs. "Love to stay and chat, mate, but fuck, I'm tired."

Sparra burst out laughing and clapped me on the shoulder. "You heard the man. Get him upstairs."

I followed Justin up, one step behind him in case he lost his balance, and grinned the whole way. That was such a Justin thing to say . . .

He sagged onto the couch and pressed the button to bring his legs up and recline, and by the time I pulled the blanket over him and kissed his forehead, he was already asleep.

I left his Squish-the-cat-proof lunch beside him and carried the rest back downstairs. Davo and Sparra were grateful for the chicken and chips, and we talked about the jobs they were working on, and inevitably they asked me if we got all the paperwork sorted out that I'd mentioned to them the day before.

"Yeah. I need to decide if we'll replace the van or maybe opt for something else," I said. "I don't know how I feel about anyone going out again." I shrugged. "I just don't know if any financial gain is worth the risk."

"Have you spoken to Jusso about it?" Davo asked.

I shook my head. "Not yet. He's had enough on his plate, and he can't even think about driving again for another three and a half months. And that's just driving. Not working on his own or going out on his own." I shrugged. "We'll see."

"If he wants to?" Sparra asked.

I sighed. "Then he can."

Davo gave a wry smile. "Yeah. And every time he drives out, you can stay here with your head between your knees in the brace position until he gets back."

I conceded a nod. "Probably." I threw my rubbish into the bin. "Did the newspaper really send someone around?"

"Yep," Davo replied. "He seemed nice enough. Didn't ask for details or nothin'. Like he didn't try and get the scoop on what Jusso's been like." He smiled. "Probably didn't fancy getting his nose broken."

I chuckled. "Smart."

"Said he'd be back tomorrow."

"Then we'll see how he fancies getting his nose broken tomorrow."

They laughed and tossed their rubbish in the bin before getting back to work. I stuck it out in the office for as long as I could stand it before I went out into the shop to help get some real work done. Well, real work that I enjoyed, anyway.

Juss came down around four, just as the boys were getting ready to leave. They chatted for a bit, then he helped me clean up and close everything down. I locked the front gate, and when I walked back into the shop, Juss was staring at his phone.

"Everything okay?"

"Still haven't heard," he said. "About the results. What if it's bad news? What if there was some medical thing from the accident, like if they gave me bad blood. Dall, I don't think I could deal with that right now."

Oh Christ. I hadn't even thought of that.

"Baby, they screen blood for all that stuff."

"It happens. I googled it."

Well, he was googling stuff now, which meant he was thinking about different things, which was a good sign. But this . . . this wasn't good. I wrapped my arms around him. "Juss, it'll be okay."

He mumbled against my chest, "What if I had some

crazy affair and got some awful STI and I can't remember him because of the accident but we found out about him from the police and he's plotting some horrible—"

I pulled back. "Justin, what did you google?"

He frowned, his face so sad. "It was something from Florida. There was a crazy lady who lost all of her memory and the police found out who she was and that she'd had an affair for years, and she fed her lover to the alligators so her husband wouldn't find out." He looked up at me, mystified. "I clicked on a link. The internet's a scary place. I mean, it has porn, which is good. But then there is some weird shit out there."

I burst out laughing and went back to hugging him. "Baby, you didn't have any affair and neither did I. There's no one else in this world but us. I promise."

He sighed. "There was a link about a guy in England who had some kind of stroke and he lost his memory, but when he woke up, he spoke French and had a different name, who turned out to be some guy that died in 1882. I don't know if he had an STI."

I snorted. "Juss, baby, it's okay." I kissed his forehead and made him look me in the eye. "But if you want to click on some crazy links, how about we do it together so you don't get freaked out."

He nodded just as my phone beeped with a message. It was the clinic, so I opened it. The rapid testing results were negative. I showed him my phone. "See? Too easy. The rest of the results will take a week."

Then his phone beeped, and he nervously handed it to me. "You read it."

I opened the message, and sure enough, the rapid test results were negative. I faced the screen to him and grinned. "Negative."

He almost sagged. "Well, that's . . . a relief."

I realised two things right then. Firstly, that'd he'd been legitimately worried over these test results and I'd downplayed his stress. And secondly, that he didn't deal with stress too well. At all.

The Juss before the accident was kinda laid back and didn't really stress too much over anything. But now he did, and I should have realised it would have affected him differently. I gave him another hug and kissed the side of his head. "You feel a bit better now, baby? I'm sorry if I didn't seem worried enough."

He nodded. "I feel better. We have another week to wait for the others, but this was the big one, right?"

"Sure. It was just the rapid test, what they pricked your finger for. They'll run a full diagnostic with the blood they drew out of your arm, and that'll take a week. But this rapid testing is pretty good." I gave him a soft kiss. "But baby, even if we got different results just now or next week, I'll still love you. Promise."

He squeezed me and nodded against my chest. "Same, Dallas. I'll still love you too." He sighed. "I just worried, and my brain was stuck on it, sorry."

"Hey, don't apologise." I pulled back and gave him a smile. "How about I make us that meatloaf for dinner?"

"Sounds great."

We finished locking up and went upstairs. Justin stayed with me in the kitchen while I made the meatloaf, so I put him to work peeling potatoes for the mash. "So," he said, "because we had unprotected blowjobs already, that means we can keep having them until we get the swab results, right?"

I stopped combining the meat mixture so I could stare at him. "Juss."

He shrugged. "I mean, if we're gonna need treatment anyway . . ."

I snorted. "Not sure that's how it works."

"But we could."

"Or we could wait. Because I should have thought of this before and not pressured you into sex without talking about testing."

He frowned. "You didn't pressure me."

"Sorry, wrong word." I stood behind him and, keeping my messy hands out, gave him a kiss on the cheek. "I still should have offered you some options."

"You did the opposite of pressure me." He put the last peeled potato on the chopping board. "And what options do you mean? Like more blowjobs?"

I chuckled. "We'll see."

"That's a yes."

It wasn't a yes, but I doubted how much I'd be able to argue with him over this. Over anything, to be honest. "How did your porn watching go this afternoon?"

He stopped and stared at me. "My porn watching . . . Oh, shit. I forgot. I was gonna spend hours catching up on Pornhub."

I chuckled. "You have a week of no sex where you can watch all the porn you want."

He gave me a cheeky smile. "Or we could watch it together. Because you did say something about options."

I laughed at that. "I kinda walked right into that, didn't I?"

He grinned victoriously, so I went back to making my meatloaf. "Dallas?" he murmured.

I turned to find him right behind me. He crooked his finger in a *come-here* motion so I leaned in closer to him thinking he wanted to whisper something in my ear, but he surprised me with a kiss to the cheek.

He didn't say anything. Just a kiss to my cheek, and it was somehow the sweetest thing ever. It made my heart bloom with love, and my stomach did that swooping free fall. I turned back to the meatloaf with the dopiest grin, and I'm pretty sure I went to bed much the same way.

---

I'D TOLD Justin about how the newspaper guy said he'd be back, but to be honest, I didn't expect him to turn up at smoko time the next day. As we got busy with work, I kinda forgot about it. But sure enough, when Davo was mastering his barista skills at the new coffee machine, Justin was helping me with a Yamaha and Sparra walked out holding a tray of Arnott's biscuits. He nodded toward the front of the workshop. "Return visitor."

A young guy had parked his car out on the street and was walking in with another guy sporting a fancy camera around his neck. They certainly didn't look like a couple of guys who rode bikes, and they weren't here to sell me anything. "Can I help you?" I asked, wiping my hands on a rag as I went to meet them.

"Samuel Cormie," the guy without the camera said, holding out his hand. "*Newcastle Times*." The other guy didn't speak.

"Ah, right," I said, shaking his hand. His hand was cold and limp, and I didn't care too much that I smeared some grease on him. "You called in yesterday."

He grinned at me, all university shine and preppy attitude. "Yeah, I was hoping to have a chat with a Mr Justin Keith if he's in today."

I normally didn't dislike anyone straight up, but knowing he was here to question Juss for shits and giggles didn't sit well with me. And as much as I wanted to tell this kid to piss right off, it wasn't my place. It was Justin's decision.

"He is. Come on through."

When he saw us, Justin got off his scooter and walked over. I didn't even get a chance to introduce them because Mr Smarmy beat me to it. He shook Juss' hand with a little too much enthusiasm. "Samuel Cormie, *Newcastle Times.*"

As soon as his hand was free, Juss wiped it on his work pants like he had to get rid of the gross feeling. It made me smile. "Justin Keith."

"I covered the accident when it happened," Cormie said. "And I was hoping I could ask you some follow-up questions on your recovery. I'm sure our readers would love to know how you're getting on."

"Uh, sure." Justin shrugged. "I guess. Not much to tell." He looked back to his scooter. "I'll just grab my wheels."

He limped back to his scooter and I went with him. "Sure you want to do this?"

"Yeah."

"Want me to stick around?"

"Nah, I got this."

"Okay, but if he asks anything about the money or compo, just say you can't speak about it."

Juss gave a nod and I left them to it, but not before giving Mr Sleazebag a look of fair warning. They walked— well, Juss scooted—out to the end of the workshop where the sun was coming through. I walked into the breakroom where I could stand and still see Justin, and Davo was chuckling.

"So you didn't like the bloke?" he asked with a laugh.

He nodded to my coffee mug, which was filled with a fresh brew.

"Thanks. And no, not much." I kept an eye out the door at where I could see Justin talking. "Do you reckon I should've stayed with him?"

"He'll be fine," Sparra said. "Let him do this."

I resisted sighing and sipped my coffee instead. I watched Juss talk for a bit. He nodded and smiled, but he kept looking my way every so often. I wanted to go to him, to see if he was okay, but Sparra was right. Juss needed to do this, to do something on his own. And by the time I'd rage-dunked several bikkies into my coffee, Mr Douche gave me a wave and hollered goodbye—I didn't care that he could see me watching the whole time —and he and his silent cameraman walked back out to their car.

Davo made Juss a decaf and had it ready for him by the time he scooted to the breakroom.

"How was it?" I asked. There was no point in trying to deny my concern. "Was he rude? Pushy?"

"Overprotective?" Davo asked with a grin.

I gave him the bird and he laughed as he walked back to the bike he was working on.

"Nah, he was okay," Juss said. "Just asked me a bunch of stuff. About my memory, of course. Apparently amnesia is interesting. And my leg and my recovery in general. Shit like that."

"We saw your photoshoot," Sparra joked.

"I told him to get the shop sign in the photo," Juss said. "Figured a promo shot couldn't hurt."

That made me smile. "As long as he wasn't a dick to you."

Sparra pushed my arm. "Dallas here watched him like a

blue heeler from the shadows. Thought he was gonna start growlin' there for a minute."

I rolled my eyes. "I just didn't want him asking anything he had no right knowing."

Sparra just laughed. "Jusso, when you're done on break, I could use a hand. Got a fuel line to replace. And Dallas ate all the Kingston biscuits."

"I did not," I shot back. "I had three."

"Sure thing," Juss replied with a laugh.

I handed him the tray of biscuits, knowing damn well he loved the plain milk bikkies and no one else would dare touch them. "You okay?"

He dunked his first biscuit. "Yeah. I know you were worried about me."

"I couldn't help it. I tried not to be."

Juss gave a smile as he dunked another biscuit and shoved it in his mouth before it could break off. "He was actually nice. He did ask about how the accident affected me financially though. I told him the accident affected everything. He didn't push me for any info."

I rubbed his arm. "Good."

He sipped his coffee. "I'm sorry I fell asleep last night."

"Don't apologise."

"I had plans. I wanted to do—" He glanced to the door to double-check no one was there. "—some things."

I chuckled. "We're supposed to wait a week."

Justin rolled his eyes. "I'm not gonna forget to watch it today. I have a whole lotta porn to catch up on. Then, by the time you finish work this arvo, I'll have had all the inspiration I need. You should probably be ready."

I barked out a laugh. "Gee, thanks. I won't be thinking about that all day or anything."

He smiled like the cat who got the cream . . . or the cat

who would get the cream later . . . Jesus. "We better get back to work."

Juss finished at lunchtime, and over the hours that followed, I tried really hard not to think about whether he was actually watching porn . . . whether or not he was jerking off to it, or maybe touching himself in other places . . .

He didn't come back down before closing time, which was a bit odd—recently he'd been coming back down to see Davo and Sparra before they left and to help me clean up—so, wondering if everything was okay, I locked everything up when the guys left and raced upstairs.

There he was, lying lengthways on the couch, propped up with pillows. He was watching something on his phone, which he pointed in my direction when I walked in. "There's a lot to catch up on. Did you know cartoon porn was a thing?"

I began to laugh as I walked over to him. I picked up Squish from Juss' side and gently put him on the floor, then very carefully lowered myself onto Juss' body. I kissed him with smiling lips. "I didn't know cartoon porn was a thing, no."

"Wanna watch it with me? There are human cartoons or animal cartoon porn. Like humans but they're animals, like horses and dogs. It's kinda weird, kinda hot. I don't wanna judge anyone," he said. I laughed as I kissed down his neck and he tilted his head, giving me more room. "Oh, I like that."

I could feel his erection, so I pulled back to look in his eyes. "Did you jerk off to it?"

His nostrils flared and his pupils blew out. "No. I wanted to wait for you."

I crushed my mouth to his and he grunted as our

tongues touched. He shifted his hips and moved his good leg so I could settle between his thighs. Our cocks were aligned, our mouths fused . . . It was glorious.

We kissed, hot and heavy, grinding and rolling our hips, feeling every nerve ending flood with desire. Juss broke the kiss, panting, his lips swollen. "You better not be playing me right now, Dall. If you tell me we should wait a week, I'll . . ."

I grinned. "You'll what?"

He growled and gnashed his teeth, nipping at my chin. "I'll . . . jerk off and finger myself and you'll only be allowed to watch."

Shock at his words and a blast of desire coursed through me. I had to push down the urge to come. "Is that so?"

"Dallas, I've just watched porn for three hours. I'm aching in a really good way and I need you to finish me."

Fuck.

I extracted myself from him, getting to my feet. A look of hurt and confusion crossed his face until I held out my hand. "Get up, and get your arse on the bed."

He grinned, and I helped him stand and followed him to our room. He stripped out of his clothes, revealing his very hard cock. Mine jerked in my briefs, dying to be free, dying for more touch, heat, and slick friction.

He sat on the bed at first, then lay down, but I pulled off my shirt and shook my head. "Roll over."

I got him comfortable with pillows under his hips to keep the pressure off his leg, and he raised his arse and stretched out like a cat. This was the old Justin. This was the pre-accident Justin who wanted to be fucked for hours, who begged for it and got pissy when he didn't get it.

"The fuck you waiting for?"

I chuckled, because that was him to a T. "Just enjoying

the view," I replied. I pulled off my boots and took off my pants, finally joining him on the bed. I knelt between his spread legs and kneaded his arse cheeks. "How does your leg feel?"

I thought for a second he was going to spit some barb at me about taking too much time, but this was a serious question. His body, his injuries, and his recovery were a priority. "Feels good."

I ran my hand up the back of his thigh and he instinctively raised his hips. "Keep still, baby. Let me do the work."

He growled at that, but he stopped moving.

I ran my hands up his back and kissed one arse cheek, then the top of his crack.

"Dallas. I'm not kidding. Stop playing. I don't know how long I can lie like this."

Okay, I didn't really think of that. "Sorry, baby. Just trying to make it feel good." I spread his arse and licked my thumb before running it over his hole.

"Holy shit, yes," he hissed.

I reached over and took the lube from the bedside and poured some to slide down his crack. He let out a long breath, and I massaged his now-slick skin. I pressed a fingertip inside him and out again, making him moan.

"Dallas," he whispered hoarsely. "More."

So I gave him more. I pushed my finger in further, sliding it in and out, and he gripped the pillow above his head. "More."

I moved my finger in circles, stretching him a little, then added a second finger. Just two fingertips and he groaned with pleasure. I pushed them in deeper, slowly in and out. I brushed his prostate and he lifted his hips.

My cock was rock hard and leaking precome. So close to

his hole, so close to where I wanted to be. But not today. Not yet.

I swiped his prostate again and I leaned my weight on his arse, as though it was my cock inside him, and I thrust my fingers in.

He bucked underneath me, crying out as he came. I thrust my fingers in a few more times, milking him as his orgasm took hold, but I needed my hand. I pulled out and gripped my own shaft, a few quick pumps, and I came so hard, shooting come onto his back.

Fucking hell. It was so intense, the room spun.

I collapsed on top of him, trying to be careful with his body, but too spent to move. My cock slid between his arse cheeks and he rolled his hips. "Just a bit lower," he whispered. "You could slide into me."

And I'd been going to ask him if he was okay. Clearly he was fine.

He rolled his hips again. "Just a little bit, Dallas. Please."

Christ almighty. I never could handle his begging. But I needed to prove to him what we had was more than physical. We needed to wait, and I had to be the strong one.

"Next time, baby."

He growled in frustration but he didn't push me. I wasn't sure I could have stopped myself if he did . . .

We lay like that for a few moments, catching our breath and enjoying the feeling of being close and naked. The full-body contact was bliss. But we were a mess, so I rolled off him and pulled him into my arms.

I kissed his forehead. "You feel okay?"

"Hmm." He was sleepy. "Yeah. Sorry for asking you to . . ."

I tightened my hold. "Don't apologise. I wanted to."

"You said next time."

I laughed and tucked him into my side, holding him tight. "You caught that, huh?"

"Sure did." He snuggled into me. "I wouldn't have minded. We got those rapid results back. And they were fine."

That was true. But still . . .

He shot back to look me in the eyes. There was hurt in his, and confusion. "Do you regret what we just did? Did you not want to do anything until—"

I cupped his face. "No, baby. Never. It was amazing and beautiful."

He sighed. "Good. 'Cause I'm not sorry. I have jizz smeared on my back, on my front, on the bed covers, on the pillows, and I'm not even remotely fucking sorry."

I laughed and pulled him against me, ending with a sigh. "I don't regret it, Juss. We were tested regularly before the accident. These tests were just to ease our minds, that's all. And like I said, the full results won't change how I feel about you. Not one thing."

He settled his head against my chest and was quiet for a long moment. "Did we do that before? I mean, me asking for you to . . . be inside me or something. Because it felt . . . familiar. I didn't remember anything, there was no flash-backs, but it felt . . . I dunno. Like my body knew what it wanted."

I gave him a squeeze. "Yeah, we did. A lot. You loved it when we'd stay like that."

"I came fast. I was thinking about it."

I chuckled. "Watching porn for a few hours had you kind of worked up."

"I'm gonna do it again tomorrow, just so you know. There's a lot of videos to get through."

I laughed again and was reminded that we were a sticky mess. "Shower time. Then you can heat up leftovers for dinner and I'll remake the bed and put these in the wash."

I helped Juss off the bed and we showered together. Then he went to sort out dinner, and I stripped the bedding and set it going in the washing machine and remade the bed with clean linen. When I went back out to the kitchen, I noticed Juss' limp was more pronounced as he took the plates to the table.

"You okay? Is your leg sore?"

"Yeah, a bit. Just time for my pills, that's all." He managed a smile. "I feel good. Great, even. A little achy in all the right places, but in a good way."

That was true. It was time for his night-time pain pills, but still . . . "You'll tell me if something hurts or gets worse though, yeah?"

He rolled his eyes as he sat down. "Yes, I promise. I am achy and tired, because I've been freshly had. But I won't object if you want to have me again."

I chuckled as I ate my first mouthful of leftover meatloaf and mash. "Your body won't be thanking me tomorrow. You might be sorer in the morning."

He made a *maybe* face but shrugged. "On the bright side, we found a position that works."

CHAPTER FIVE

TWO DAYS LATER, all the insurance money had hit my account. I paid off all the credit cards and put a chunk on the overdraft, feeling like things were finally—finally— starting to be okay. It was one thing knowing the money troubles would be over soon, but it was a whole other thing to know it was *actually* over.

The bank account was looking pretty fat, Juss was more himself, and life was looking pretty damn good.

Until Davo came into work and handed me a folded copy of the *Times*. "Jusso's interview is on page three. There's a photo of the crash. Not sure if you want him to see it."

My stomach dropped. "Thanks, mate."

Davo gave a hard nod and went out and made a point of having a chat with Sparra and Juss, probably so I could have a quick look and decide how best to prepare Justin. He'd seen some insurance photos as part of the van claim, but nothing too graphic.

I turned to page three, my heart in my throat. There were two photos: one of Justin just a few days ago, and one of the mangled van. The photo of him was on his right side, getting a good look at the scar down his head. I remember Juss saying he wanted to get the name of the shop in it, and it was . . . but the photographer knew what he was doing. The picture emphasised his scar more than anything else.

The photo of the van was one the paper had run after the accident. The van was barely separated from the truck, the door was missing from where they'd obviously had to cut him out. It was . . . crumpled, smashed, barely recognisable. There was debris all over the wet road, glass, pieces of metal. It looked like a war zone.

God, it made me feel sick.

Then I read the article.

---

**Memories Erased**

Justin Keith's life changed forever on that rainy morning almost four months ago when the van he was driving was hit by a truck. Taken to John Hunter Hospital, he was rushed into surgery for a serious head injury, multiple broken bones and fractures to his skull.

Not that he remembered any of it.

Because a few days later when he woke up, Justin thought he was five years younger and still living in Darwin. He'd lost the last five years of his life. He had no memory of his job, his home, and no memory of the four-year relationship with his partner.

Justin was diagnosed with retrograde amnesia, a

condition which affects memory. But it's more than that, Justin says.

"I didn't just lose the memories. I lost all the emotional connections from the last five years as well. I lost who I was and where I fit in. Where I belonged."

A motorbike mechanic by trade, Justin says getting back to work was paramount to his recovery. "I couldn't tell you who the Prime Minister is or who won the last five footy premierships or even where I lived. But I could pull a bike engine apart and put it back together again, no worries. I know bikes, and doing work that I knew by heart really helped remind me who I was."

Justin says he's limited by what he can do. "I can only do a few hours in the mornings, then it gets too much. My brain can't do what it used to, and my leg and arm don't work like they should. And I still have a lot of doctor appointments, and headaches are a constant part of my life now."

He's recovered a few memories, but only pieces. "Amnesia isn't like the movies. It's awful. I remember a few things, like flashes or random stuff. I feel robbed. My leg and arm will heal, but I've lost those memories, probably forever."

It hasn't been easy on his relationships. "I've been real lucky to have such good people in my life who've stuck by me." His smile brightens. "And I got to fall in love for the first time. Again. I don't remember the first time."

Traumatic brain injury is a leading cause of disability in Australia, with links to violence, homelessness and suicide. In fact, many people who suffer serious TBI end up in care homes or in long-term care, and there have been links to other cognitive degeneration in later years.

Investigations into the crash concluded it was an accident, and the matter was settled for an undisclosed amount.

"Nothing is like it was. Everything is different. But I'm alive and I have plans for the future, so maybe I'm one of the lucky ones."

---

I SWALLOWED hard as I considered what Justin had said. None of it was a surprise to me—I knew all of that—though I did smile at the falling in love again comment . . . But I had to wonder if the comment about the undisclosed amount was just a general wrap-up or if that smarmy reporter knew. At any rate, I'm glad no figure was noted.

Now I just had to break it to Justin. It wasn't like I could shield him from this, or even if I should. I was just weary of the fallout, how he would react, and if it might upset him and set him back a day or two.

I could hear the boys talking in the breakroom, laughing about the coffee machine or something. I picked up the newspaper and went in. Justin grinned when he saw me and pointed to my now-full coffee mug. He was playing barista today, apparently, which probably explained the laughter.

I held up the newspaper. "Your interview."

"Oh." His smile wavered and his eyes met mine. "Is it okay? Is something wrong?"

"No. There's just a photo of the van, after the crash, if you're ready to see it."

He stared at me for a long second, his eyes full of determination; then he gave a nod. "I'm ready."

He took the newspaper and sat at the table, and when he looked up, Davo had dragged Sparra out, leaving just me. I sat down beside him and waited.

Justin looked at the photo of the van. He shook his head like he couldn't believe it and chewed his bottom lip. I slid my hand over his and squeezed, just to let him know I was there. I wasn't going anywhere.

He nodded to let me know he was okay.

We didn't need to speak. We just knew.

"Wow," he whispered, staring at the photograph. "Was that what the van looked like? I don't remember it at all. Not before the accident, certainly not like that . . ." He let out a low breath. "Jesus."

"You okay?"

He nodded again, giving me a small smile. "Yeah. Not surprising I got messed up though, is it?"

I didn't want to say he was lucky, because telling him that, after all his injuries and memory loss, would be just insulting. "It could have been so much worse, Juss. We could have lost you that day."

Then he squeezed my hand and studied me for a second. "Are you okay? Seeing this picture?"

Him asking me that made me smile, but I looked at the photograph again. "I'm okay, baby. Just thankful I still have you."

He leaned over and gave me a soft kiss, then went back to the newspaper. "This photo's okay," he said, pointing to the picture of him. He smiled proudly. "Got the shop name in it."

It also got the huge scar that snaked down the side of his head, but I didn't say that. "He's cute."

He smiled again, then began to read the article. He didn't read too fast now, so I just held his hand, giving him all the time he needed.

He nodded when he was done and pushed the newspaper away. "Did it read okay?" he asked. "Did I sound okay? I know sometimes I don't talk great."

"Hey, baby, you were perfect," I replied, turning to face him and holding his hand in both of mine. "You sounded great, and you talk just fine. Don't worry about what anyone else thinks. You're doing better than the docs ever thought possible, so give yourself some credit, baby."

He made a face but conceded a smile. "You have to say that."

I snorted. "I don't *have* to say anything. I said it because it's true." I traced a line on his palm. "And you said you got to fall in love again."

His eyes met mine. "Because I did."

"I love you too, Juss."

"Well, I better get some work done," he said. He tried to smile but it didn't quite sit right.

"You sure you're okay?" I asked. "If you're mad or upset about the article or the photo, you can tell me."

He frowned. "I don't know how I feel about it," he admitted. And that was a good start. Last time he bottled stuff up, it messed with him for days. His brain couldn't handle the overthinking right now.

"That's okay, Juss. That's good. Take your time, think some more on it, and see how you feel," I suggested. "We can talk about it later."

He nodded, relieved. His smile was more genuine this time. "Thanks."

I stood and pulled him to his feet. He drank half his now-warm coffee and tipped the rest down the sink. I drank mine and followed him out to the workshop. Juss headed straight for Sparra—he was helping him with a Honda—and Davo gave me a nod to come over.

"How is he?" he asked.

"He's okay. Still not sure. He needs some time to think about it. But thanks for giving me the heads up about it first."

"No worries," he said.

We went about our work as per normal. It was busy: customers, the usual bookings, phone calls, suppliers. And when we stopped for smoko, Justin said he might, if it was all right with me, call it a day.

"Headache's not getting much better," he said.

"Yeah, of course," I replied. "Go on up and rest. I'll order some lunch in for everyone today and bring it up later."

He gave a nod and took the stairs one at a time, and I knew the newspaper article was playing on his mind.

"Is he okay?" Sparra asked. "He's been quiet this morning."

"Yeah. He'll be okay." I sighed. "But I feel like calling that fucking newspaper reporter dickhead and telling him to add this part of Justin's amnesia to his story. That some little interview piece for ratings will fuck Juss up for a day. How seeing that photograph would mess with the way his brain's wired. Stress and bullshit do a real number on him now."

"Yeah," Davo agreed. "He looked kinda spaced."

I nodded, and it got the better of me. "I might just go up and check on him." I got to the breakroom door. "Save me a Kingston."

I took the stairs two at a time and opened the door as quiet as I could. He wasn't on the couch, so I stuck my head around the bathroom door, but it was empty too. That left the bedroom. I peeked inside, and there he was in bed lying on his side, his boots on the floor, the covers pulled up, and Squish curled up at his stomach. Juss was stroking Squish's neck, his eyes almost closed.

"Hey, baby," I whispered as I came in. I sat beside him and put my hand on his arm. "You okay?"

"Just feel . . . awful."

I stroked his hair, feeling his forehead as I did. He didn't feel hot. "Can I get you your pills?"

"Nah. Just need some sleep. Tired. Headache. Same old."

I frowned, hating that this was his new normal. "Okay, I'll leave you to rest. I just wanted to make sure you were okay."

He slow blinked. "Didn't mean to make you worry."

I leaned down and kissed his temple. "I will always worry." I noticed his phone on the bedside. "Call me if you need anything."

His eyes closed and he hummed. "'Kay."

I gave Squish a pat too, and he purred louder. "Look after him, Squish. You're in charge."

The corner of Juss' mouth lifted, just a touch. And with another brush of Juss' hair, I left them both to sleep.

Work got busy for the next few hours, but I did remember to order some pizzas for lunch, for which Davo and Sparra were very grateful. I took some upstairs for Juss, not sure if he'd even be awake, but he was. He was on the couch now, changed out of his work gear and wearing trackies and a hoodie, though he was mostly hidden under a blanket. The TV wasn't on, but he was looking at something on his phone, and Squish, as always, was purring beside him.

"Pizza delivery," I said, putting the box next to him. "How are you feeling?"

He put his phone down. "Okay. Better. Drugs kicked in."

"Good." I knew his meds made him drowsy and spacey, but it had to be better than searing pain. I grabbed us a bottle of water each from the fridge and slid his next to the pizza box. I helped myself to a slice and sat at the other end of the couch. "Can I see you at least eat a piece?"

Justin rolled his eyes and let his head fall back onto the headrest, but he didn't say anything.

"What?" I asked with a smile. "You want to tell me to piss off?"

His gaze went to mine.

"You're allowed to be pissed off or frustrated with me," I added. "I know I'm pushy."

Juss sighed. "I don't mean it."

"I know." I took another bite of the pizza, chewed, and swallowed. "But those pills make you nauseous if you don't eat."

He sighed again, with more bite this time. "I'm not a kid."

"No, you're not."

He scowled at the wall for a bit, but his grumpy face softened. "Thank you for bringing me food."

I smiled at him. "You're welcome."

Now he pouted. "And thank you for checking up on me."

I stood up and, leaning down, kissed his forehead. "Any time. I'll leave you to rest."

"You don't have to go. I didn't mean to make you feel unwelcome."

"No, it's fine. I better get back down there and steal a

piece of the Supreme before Davo eats it all." The truth was, I reckoned Juss would eat a piece or two of pizza and sleep hard for a few more hours yet. He was still tired. And I had work that needed doing. "Make sure Squish doesn't steal any pizza."

Juss managed half a smile before I got to the door, but I wasn't wrong in my prediction. He ate and slept a while longer, though he did come back down to the shop for a bit before closing time. He still wore his track pants and hoodie, but he found the broom and put it to work, keeping busy though mostly keeping to himself.

At knock-off time, Davo pulled the roller door down, the sound giving a metallic rumbling finality to the week. Thank God it was the weekend. "Hey, you still wanna grab a drink at the Arms tomorrow? It's all right if you wanna leave it."

"What's that?" Juss asked, overhearing.

Had I asked him this? I was going to, then we'd just got sidetracked. "Wanna meet the boys at the pub tomorrow? We can grab a feed and watch the footy. We don't have to stay long."

Juss, still holding the broom, looked from me to Davo and Sparra, then back to me. "Sure. Sounds good."

He was still a bit off. His expression was flat and his eyes didn't shine when he smiled. The boys probably thought it was just the meds, if they noticed it at all, but I knew him.

He had something on his mind, something was bothering him and weighing him down. I was certain it was that damn photograph, and I was so grateful it was closing time on a Friday so me and him could just chill out on the couch and talk.

"See ya's tomorrow at four," I said, waving Davo and Sparra off.

"It's your shout, remember?" Sparra called back with a grin.

I laughed. "I haven't forgotten." I locked the gate behind them and went back into the workshop, ready to close everything down. "Thank God it's the weekend."

Juss walked right up to me and into a hug. I held him warm and tight, rubbed his back, and kissed his head. "You ready to go upstairs?" I murmured.

He nodded. "Yeah."

I closed my office door, and when I went to shut the breakroom door, I noticed the damn newspaper. I picked it up and aimed it for the bin, but Juss stopped me. "No, keep it."

"You sure?"

He nodded again. "I dunno what for. Just don't want to throw it out."

I frowned but wasn't about to argue. "Okay then, let's go home."

That made him smile. "Sounds good."

I turned everything off and made sure everything was locked, and we went upstairs. Justin went to the kitchen and leaned against the counter, his arms folded. Then he went through the fridge, not finding what he wanted, then he put the kettle on, and then he cleared off the table before he straightened up the couch cushions.

"Baby, what's wrong?"

He stopped and leaned against the back of the couch and folded his arms again. Then he shoved his hands in the pockets of his hoodie, and when that wasn't right, he folded his arms again. I went to him and unpeeled his arm away and held his hand.

"Was it the photograph?"

He looked away and squinted. "Not really. A bit, but . . ."

I put my hand to his cheek and gently turned him so he'd look at me. "Then what is it?"

"What he said, at the end."

I tried to remember . . . "The undisclosed amount of money?"

He shook his head. "No. The part about the brain injuries." When it was clear I couldn't remember, he frowned. "The part where he said that people like me end up in a home."

Wait, what? "Juss, I don't . . ."

He went to the table where I'd put the newspaper and found the article. "Here. 'Traumatic brain injury is a leading cause of disability in Australia, with links to violence, homelessness, and suicide. In fact, many people who suffer serious TBI end up in care homes or in long-term care, and there have been links to other cognitive degeneration in later years.'" He looked at me. "Did you not read that part?"

"I did, but I . . ." I shook my head, flustered. "I didn't apply it to you. I just read it as statistics for the article. I . . . I should have taken more notice. Sorry."

He stared, bewildered and stunned. "How does it not apply to me? Dallas, how does that not apply to me?"

"Because it doesn't. I dunno! I would never let you get put into a care home. Jesus, Justin. Never."

"But you can't say that. Because you don't know."

"I do know that." I went to him and cupped his face. "I wouldn't."

He chewed on his bottom lip. "I know. It's just . . ." He sighed. "This afternoon, since I read that article, I've been reading up on the long-term effects of TBI. What it will mean for me when I'm fifty, sixty. It's not good, Dallas. I'll be more prone to dementia or stroke. My brain is . . . damaged."

I lifted his chin so he'd look into my eyes. "You listen to me. Your brain is part of you, who you are. I love *all* of you. And I promise you, Justin, I will love you at fifty and sixty, seventy, or one hundred, God willing. There are no guarantees what will happen between now and then. Hell, something could happen to me next week."

"Dallas . . ."

"No. Justin, no. There are no guarantees. And it doesn't matter to me if you have some long-term effects. It won't ever change how I feel about you. If things got worse or bad and I couldn't look after you like you needed, I'd hire someone to help me. But I wouldn't send you away."

"Didn't you hear what I said?"

"What?"

"Dementia, Dallas," he said with tears in his eyes. "Dementia! What if I can't remember you again? You can't go through that again. I saw how much it hurt you, how the light left your eyes when I didn't know who you were. Knowing that might happen again just kills me. It fucking kills me."

*Oh no, no, no . . .*

"Baby, we'll get through it. If and when that ever happens, we'll deal with it. But we can't worry about that now. If we have thirty years before we need to start dealing with that shit, then let's make the most out of those thirty years. Let's not waste a minute worrying about something that might not ever happen."

"I don't want to get dementia," he said, letting his tears

fall. "I don't want to lose my memories again. I've lost enough. I've lost—" He couldn't speak for crying.

I pulled him into my arms and let him cry. He needed to cry for everything he'd lost, for everything that had been taken from him. To grieve for what was gone and in fear of what his future might hold. When he'd caught his breath, I kissed the side of his head. "Sweetheart, who knows what medical advancements they'll have in twenty or thirty years. You don't have to worry about it now, my love. And even if it is something we need to deal with, we'll deal with it together." I held him a little tighter and rubbed his back. "I'm sorry I didn't pick up on that part of the newspaper article."

He pulled back a little, his face still downcast, his eyes red and puffy. "I just started to think of the future, ya know? I hadn't thought about anything past the next few minutes in so long, like I'd forgotten the future was even a thing. Then you mentioned it the other day. You said it sounded like I was starting to think of the future, and I was. And now I find out that my future's been taken away too." His bottom lip trembled. "It's not fair."

"I know it's not. It isn't fair, and it shouldn't have happened to you. I hate that it happened to you. But I promise we'll work it out. Whatever life throws at us, we'll tackle it together."

He nestled his head against my chest. "I couldn't do this without you."

"And I couldn't do it without you, Juss. So we're even."

"Yes, you could. You'd cope all right. Me, on the other hand . . . I wouldn't have a home or a job. I couldn't get anywhere or do anything. I can't even go to the supermarket without needing a nap afterwards."

"Baby, you don't ever have to worry about being without me, okay?"

He didn't reply.

"Hey," I said. "You wanna know what real love is?"

"What's that?" he mumbled into my chest.

"Real love is hard. And sometimes it hurts. Sometimes we need to change what was our normal course and take a different path. Sometimes everything we knew becomes something different, and we need to adapt. There might be medical appointments and we might have to change the way we shop for groceries or if we go out for lunch. But that's just what we do because that's what love is. It's not all roses and sunshine. It's laundry and dishes, bills and mortgages, and wet towels on the floor, or changing the cat litter. We adapt and we roll with it. So all these changes that we've had to deal with because of the accident, I don't mind one bit, Juss. Because when I fell in love with you, it was forever. In health and in sickness, or however that goes."

He chuckled, just for a half a second, then sniffled into my shirt.

"And you wanna know what else love is?" I went on. "It's amazing and wonderful. It gives me strength and hope, and it makes me realise there's more to my life than just me. Falling in love with you, Juss, was the single best thing to ever happen to me. Ever. I was feeling kinda lost until you came into my life."

He pulled back and lifted his head to look at me. "You were?"

I nodded. "Yep. Work kept me busy for a long time, but I'd meet guys who were just not right for me. They were either all about fitness or money or partying, and I wasn't interested. Then you came along, perfect in every way for me." Then I gave him a wink. "Except the fact you were a Knights supporter. But I forgive you for that."

He finally smiled. Finally.

"What I'm trying to say, Juss, is that love has its ups and downs. But you and me, we got this. We found each other years ago, and when the universe tried to pull us apart with the accident, we found each other again."

He got a little teary again, but he still smiled. "I love you so much," he whispered.

I kissed him softly. "I know."

## CHAPTER SIX

JUSS WAS adamant about going out to the pub with the guys. After our talk about the possibility of him getting dementia when he was older, we'd had dinner and spent the night snuggled up on the couch with Juss as the little spoon. I'd watched the footy, but Juss rolled over and faced me, snuggled into my chest for most of the game. He dozed on and off, but clearly, his day of anguish had taken its toll.

We'd gone to bed after that and he'd slept right through, so he'd woken up feeling better. I mean, he was still his usual grouchy-morning self, but he was feeling less insecure about his future.

Which was why he was adamant we go out with the guys. He wanted to enjoy all that he could now. Like I'd said last night, we should make the most of every minute of every day, and going out and being sociable, even for a little while, gave him a real sense of normalcy. So after breakfast and showers, we went downstairs to get some odds and ends done in the office, and overall it was a productive morning, without overdoing it. Juss even wanted to go back upstairs and rest for a bit before we went so he wouldn't be too tired.

"Because it's what we do now," he said with a fond smile and a roll of his eyes.

I grinned at him using my words against me. "It sure is."

So while he dozed off for a bit, I got some laundry done and cleaned the bathroom, doing all that boring housework stuff that needed doing. I didn't mind doing it all now because I had every intention of coming home when we left the pub and spending the entire night as the big spoon on the couch again.

I wanted to do that every night for the rest of my life.

Just me and Juss, forever.

I refused to believe that he'd end up with dementia or some other degenerative disease. Okay, so maybe not *refused to believe*. Because I did believe that shit was possible. But I refused to live in fear of it. I didn't want it to rob us of *now*, with worry and fear. I didn't want him stressing over something that was possibly decades away.

This whole thing had taught me to appreciate every second of *now*.

I thought he might have a change of heart as we were getting ready to go, but if anything, he was more excited. He even put on a pair of jeans for the first time since his accident. I had to help him get his foot through the leg hole, but he smiled when he got them done up. "Feel fancy," he said as he buttoned up his shirt. "Been a while since I wore anything but trackies and work pants."

I looked at his reflection. "You look great."

He smiled back at me. "So do you. I've seen photos of you all dressed up, but I've never seen you . . . I mean, I don't remember it."

Jeans and a button-down shirt were hardly dressed up, but I guess to him it was when the only outfits he could remember were tracksuits and dirty work clothes. "My jeans are feeling a little tight, not gonna lie."

I turned to check out my backside in the mirror and was reminded of all the running I hadn't done in the last three months. Justin looked down at my legs and raked his eyes up my body. "Yeah, no. I reckon you fill them out just right."

I laughed and gave him a quick kiss before I pulled on my boots, helped Juss with his, and grabbed our coats. I took the cane, which lived behind the front door, and Juss sighed but didn't say anything. Squish was curled up on Juss' blanket on the couch, so we left him in charge and made our way to the pub.

It was a quick drive, though when we got there, the car park was almost full and the walk to the pub was uneven. I handed him the walking cane, and he took it with a roll of his eyes. "I hate this," he grumbled.

"You'd hate tripping or injuring your leg even more," I replied. He took a few steps with it. "Does it hurt your arm to use it?"

"Nah. It's okay. If I was sitting on the ground, I wouldn't like to have to use my arm to get up, like to take all my weight, but like this it isn't too bad." He actually walked pretty good with the cane. He wasn't gonna win any gold medals in a speed-walking contest, but that was okay with me.

I held the door for him and he gave me a cute smile as he walked in. "Thank you," he said.

"You're welcome," I whispered back. I followed him, and once we were in the main bar area, he stopped.

"Do you know where they are?"

It occurred to me then that he had no memory of this place. He'd been here many times, but he'd lost all that.

"There's a bar out the back with tables and seats and a huge screen for the footy."

"Ah." He turned to the end of the bar area but didn't move.

"This way," I said, leading the way. It was busy. Not overcrowded but enough that people edged out of Justin's way when they saw him with the cane to give him room to walk through.

Sure enough, Davo and Lauren and Sparra and his new girlfriend were seated at a round table with two spare seats. Davo gave us a wave when he saw us. "Hey," he said. "Was wondering where you two were."

"We're not even late," I said.

"Footy's about to start."

In about an hour, but whatever. "Then I better get to the bar," I said, grinning. I said hello to Lauren and smiled at the new face. "Hi."

Sparra stood up. He'd obviously put an effort into his appearance, and he even looked a little nervous. "Dallas, this is Carissa. And Justin. Carissa, my girlfriend." He just about beamed at the word.

Carissa was short and curvy, with pastel pink hair and a stud in her nose. She had huge blue eyes and a killer smile. She stood and shook our hands. "Nice to meet you. Tony talks about you all the time."

"Nice to meet you too," I replied.

"Tony?" Justin asked. "Oh, Sparra's real name. I forgot, sorry. What the hell kind of name is Tony?"

They all laughed, and I pulled out the seat next to Sparra for Juss and he sat down, hanging the cane handle over the edge of the table. "Okay, it's my shout. What are we having?"

I took their orders and made my way to the bar, ordering

for everyone. It was probably long overdue that I shouted these guys a few drinks. I tucked some menus under my arm and carried the tray of drinks back to the table. I got two Carlton Zeros for me and Juss. It was non-alcoholic but it looked and tasted like a beer, and I hoped it made Juss feel like he wasn't missing out.

He took the bottle and shot me a look before reading the label. He gave it a sceptical once over, then took a sip. "I haven't had beer in . . . well, I can't remember having a beer in five years, and this actually tastes pretty good."

Sparra clinked his bottle to Juss' and said, "Cheers, mate. And it's good to have you here."

I sat between Juss and Davo and we chatted about the menus, and once everyone had decided, I went to the bistro counter and ordered and paid for that too.

"You don't have to do that," Davo said. He'd come with me to the service counter to collect the cutlery and condiments.

"I know. I want to. As thanks for what you and Sparra have done, but also as a bit of a celebration. This is Juss' first time going out somewhere for a meal. Like to a restaurant type thing and to watch the footy. He usually falls asleep on the couch watching with me at home."

"I wasn't sure if you'd be here, given he didn't have a real good day yesterday."

"Yeah, he's okay. He's just no good if he bottles stuff up. His brain trips a circuit if he gets stressed. But we talked it out and he slept it off."

"Good." Then Davo nudged me. "Have you ever seen Sparra scrubbed up like that? He's on his best behaviour. Showered and shaved and everything."

I chuckled. "Ah, bless him. She seems nice."

"He's a goner already," Davo said. "Smitten kitten."

I snorted. "How's Lauren? Keeping you in line, no doubt."

"She's great. She's, uh . . ." He looked around, still holding a bunch of forks. "She's pregnant. Six weeks. Don't tell anyone. I'm not supposed to tell anyone."

*Holy shit.* "Oh my God, Davo," I tried to whisper. "That is such good news. The best news."

He nodded, his smile proud. "Yeah, we're pretty happy."

I could see that. Man, that was just the kind of news we needed. Something wonderful to look forward to. "I'm really happy for you. And if you need any time off for appointments or whatever it is—" I waved a wad of serviettes. "—they do. You just say the word."

He looked back over to the table, where Lauren was watching us. She sipped her lemonade, and with a smile, she shook her head. She knew he was telling me. I laughed and gave him a nudge. "You're in trouble now."

Davo hadn't stopped smiling yet. "Always."

We went back to our table and we finished our meals just before the footy started. "I better get some more drinks," I said. "Juss, you want another or something else?"

"Yeah, I'll have another one of these," he said, draining the last of his bottle. He was all smiles and laughter, no alcohol required. He was just happy to be out and socialising with his friends. And it didn't help that Carissa was also a Knights supporter.

My God, it made me happy to see him smiling like that.

And we watched the footy, and we laughed like we hadn't in months. But it was loud and busy, and I could see Juss was getting tired. The noise had to be killing his head. I squeezed his thigh. "You ready to go?"

He gave me a nod. "Need to pee first." He looked around. "Where's the loo?"

I gave him his cane. "It's just through those double doors on your left." There was a small step into the bathrooms . . . "You know, I can show you."

"I got him," Sparra said. "Need to go shake a leg anyway."

They walked off and I watched, of course. "He'll be fine," Davo said.

"Can't help it," I admitted. If he fell or got dizzy . . .

"He looks good, Dallas," Lauren said. "Dave's been keeping me up to date with how he's going. Bit scary there for a while, huh?"

"Frightening," I agreed. "But he's getting better every day."

"And his memory?" she asked, hopeful.

I shook my head. "Not much, snippets here and there. Nothing new this week. He can't remember this place at all."

She frowned. "I can't even imagine."

"To be honest, neither can I. I dunno what I'd do if it were me in his shoes," I admitted.

"You'd be right where he is, only it'd be him looking after you," Davo said. "No questions asked."

I almost smiled. "Probably. You should have seen his face when I told him I'm a Bulldog supporter. He was horrified."

They were still laughing when Sparra and Juss came back. Juss didn't sit down, so I stood. "You ready?"

He nodded and slow blinked. But he gave them a smiley wave. "I gotta tap out," he said. He smiled to Carissa and Lauren. "Nice to meet you. And I'll see you boys at work."

After a round of goodbyes, we made our way back out

through the bar. Juss was leaning on the cane more, evidence of his tiredness. "Wanna stay here and I'll bring the ute closer?"

"Nah," he said, still smiling. We made our way through the car park, real slow and steady, until we reached the ute. I opened his door for him and helped him get in, then got into my seat and helped him do up his seatbelt. "Had a real good day, Dall."

I leaned over the console and gave him a quick kiss. "Me too, baby."

He was asleep before we got out of the car park, and when we got home, he was too drowsy to climb the stairs. "I'll carry you," I said, helping him out of the car.

"Mm," he said, clinging to my neck. "This way."

"Okay, hold on," I said, then put my hands on his arse and hoisted him up onto my hips, like a front-ways piggy-back. "You gotta hold on, baby."

He used his left arm to hold the back of my neck, but his right arm wasn't much good, and his left leg went around me, but I had to be careful of his right leg. It wasn't exactly easy, but step by step, I got him up the stairs and through the door. Except when I went to put his feet on the floor, he snuggled his face into my neck, hung on tighter, and refused to get down.

I thought about setting his arse on the kitchen counter, because it was closer, and then the couch, but it was too low. So I walked him into our room and gently lowered him onto the bed. He pulled me down with him and I had to be careful not to land on his leg or bump his head.

He was all smiles, his eyes closed, and he hooked his left leg around me and locked me on top of him. I was going to say something or kiss him or laugh, but he was already asleep.

JUSS WAS PRETTY WIPED for most of Sunday. I did a groceries run in the morning and we took a drive in the afternoon to the beach to soak up some rays. He took his scooter because the pathways at the beach were long-and-wide smooth concrete.

Justin opted for shorts because his legs were paler than pale, and spring was coming to Newcastle so the sun was warm, but I threw in a hoodie because the breeze off the Pacific still had some bite.

He didn't care if people saw the scars on his leg. The fact he used a mobility scooter and had a huge scar down the side of his head kept them staring enough. But he was still in a good mood from yesterday.

"What have we got on this week?" he asked.

We were lying on a blanket on the grass before the sand, staring up at the bluest sky, holding hands. "Just a workday tomorrow, but Tuesday we have your physio appointment and then your session with Doctor Chang. We have to be there by eight. We can go out for breakfast before if you want, have some fancy eggs benny. Or after."

"Sounds good."

"Rest of the week is pretty normal. You got that scan next week though."

He smiled at me before he turned back to the sky. "I hate that MRI machine. And they inject me with that stuff."

"Just think, you've got this next scan appointment, then you've only gotta go in every two weeks instead."

"Thank God."

"And no more scans for another three months." It was hard to believe it had been three months already . . .

He was quiet for a bit. "They say six months is about the

cut-off," he said. "For memories to come back. If they haven't come back by then, chances are they're not coming back."

I squeezed his hand. "I wish I knew what to say, Juss. I know you want them back, and I hate that they were taken away. But we get to make new ones."

"Like this? Lying here, holding hands, and staring at the sky?"

"Yep."

"Is this like date number six or something? I think I've lost count."

"We can go back to one if you want. Dinner, candles, a movie."

He chuckled. "No. No more back-to-square-one bullshit. We can go with date number six, right?"

"Hell yes, we can." I laughed. "We can do that tonight if you want. I bought steak for dinner. I'll let you pick the movie."

"Something funny."

"*Deadpool.*"

"Dead-what?"

I laughed. "Oh, baby. You are in for a treat."

------

WE ARRIVED at Justin's physio appointment on Tuesday morning with his cane in hand. He wasn't a fan of it, but it was easier to use and he was far more mobile now. This would also be his last weekly physio appointment, moving into the fortnightly slots with his other appointments. His MRI scheduled for next week meant no physio and Juss wasn't mad about missing it. He did all his exercises regularly, and physically, he was doing great.

Doctor Chang was her usual happy self, pleased with all of Justin's progress. He'd had no new memories this week, and she reassured us that that didn't mean Justin wouldn't recover any memories ever again. His focus was improving and his cognitive connections were too. Overall, he was improving every day. He told her about the newspaper article and how the insurance was a relief. Then he mentioned what he'd read online about the likelihood of getting dementia, and with a reassuring smile, Doctor Chang had discussed medical research and reassured him with facts and statistics.

He was relieved; I could tell by the set of his shoulders. When we sat at the café and ordered our brunch, I gave his hand a squeeze. "Feeling better now?"

He smiled but rolled his eyes. "Yes, but it's still not fair that you know everything I'm thinking just by looking at me."

I laughed. "Wanna know what else I know?"

"What's that?"

"That it's been a week. We should be getting our full clinic test results back today or tomorrow."

His smile widened and his left eyebrow shot up. "Now that *is* good news. Well, if we get a green light, it's good news. If they tell me I need more tests and I need to wait longer, then that will be bad news, and . . ." His eyes shot to mine, panicked. "Dall, what if they tell me—"

I squeezed his hand firmly. "Then we do whatever they tell us to do, and if we have to wait, we wait." I gave him a nudge. "Not that we've exactly abstained anyway. And the rapid testing is usually the only tests a lot of people do. We were just being extra cautious."

He hummed as he sipped his decaf, then cleared his

throat and shifted in his seat. "Do you think the mail will have been delivered by now?"

I chuckled and checked my watch. "Yep."

Juss looked around for the waitress. "Where the hell is our food?"

I laughed, and admittedly, we ate our meals pretty quick. I managed not to speed on the way home, though my mind was now on one thing . . .

We were only a block from the shop when my phone rang. The call from work came through my Bluetooth. "Hello?" I answered.

"Hey, Dall." It was Davo. "How far away are you?"

"Just around the corner. Why?"

"Someone's here to see Jusso. Pretty sure he's not gonna like it."

I frowned and Juss looked at me, worried. *What the fuck?* "Davo, we're just pulling in." I ended the call and turned into the shop, driving around the back. There was an old silver car in the customer parking, but I didn't recognise it.

I pulled up around the back and helped Juss out of the ute. Davo met us at the roller door. "I'm sorry," he said. "I didn't know what to say. She's in the breakroom and wouldn't leave until you got back."

She . . .

We went inside, Juss using his cane and me close by his side. And sure enough, like a bad, bad dream, sat the one person who could topple everything. With her emotionless eyes and forced smile, the bitch didn't even stand up.

Juss froze. "Mum?"

## CHAPTER SEVEN

"WHAT ARE YOU DOING HERE?" Juss asked warily. He was barely in the doorway, a safe distance from his mother. Janet had short dark-brown greying hair, hard eyes, and her lips were pressed into a constant thin line. She wore some hideous grey tracksuit pants and white sneakers that looked plastic. Her sweater was pink, and also hideous, but the look on her face . . . her contempt made her fake smile a sneer.

"Thought I'd come and see you. Rebecca told me about the accident." She looked him up and down, giving the walking cane a once over. "You seem okay now."

I bristled, and maybe I growled because both Juss and his mother looked at me. I was too angry to speak.

"I see you're still . . . ," she said, waving her hand to the both of us, her fake smile tight and uneasy.

"Still gay, still together," I bit out. "Shall we just go with whichever one you hate the most?"

She sneered, but Juss put his hand on my arm. "I got this."

She shot me a satisfied smirk, and I wanted to pull her off that chair and throw her the fuck out of my shop.

Juss limped in and pulled out a chair. He gently lowered himself into it and kept his cane between his legs. I stood in the doorway with my arms crossed, and Justin smiled up at me before patting the chair next to him. "Sit with me, Dall."

Janet's smirk died, and at least *that* made me smile. Juss turned back to his mother. "I'm still not sure what you're doing here," he said. "The accident was three months ago."

"Becca said you needed time to recover," she said, as if that was a justifiable excuse.

"I almost died," he said, turning his head and pointing to his scar. "It's called traumatic brain injury. I was in hospital for weeks and you never even called."

"I know we didn't leave on very good terms last time," she began.

"Justin doesn't remember the last time we saw you," I explained. "But I do. I remember the names you called him, the names you called me. I remember how you told us we were going to hell and how disgusting we are. He doesn't remember." I poked my finger into my chest. "But I fucking do."

Juss frowned at me. "You said she didn't say nice things. Is that what she said?"

I shook my head. "I didn't want to upset you. And I'm sorry, Juss."

She pursed her lips and sniffed. "I was angry. And I didn't say it like that."

I stared at her, stunned that she'd deny it.

"I remember when you told me those things when I came out, and again before I moved to Darwin," Juss said.

"So if Dallas says that's what you said another time, then I believe him."

She cleared her throat and spoke like she didn't care about what Justin had just said. "Well, I was hoping we could get past that."

I realised then what she was doing here. Or, more to the point, *why* she was here.

"Jesus fucking Christ," I said, disgusted. "I want you to leave."

She shot me an affronted look. "I'm allowed to speak to my son."

I ignored her and turned to Justin. "Juss, she wants your money."

"My what?" he asked quietly.

"Your money. She read the newspaper article that said there was an undisclosed sum of money from the insurance. That's why she's here."

Juss stared at me, his eyes wide with shock and sadness. He was already tired, and now this was gonna send him into a spin. I could see it in his eyes.

He turned to her and the bitch didn't even try to dispute it. "I just thought we could chat, Jussy."

I fucking bristled again. "Don't even fucking start, and get the fuck out of my shop."

"You can't make me leave. I'm allowed to talk to my son."

"You didn't want to speak to him in the last five years or the two years before that. Or before that. Or when he was lying in a hospital bed, close to dying. Where were you for any of his surgeries or physiotherapy or his weekly medical appointments?" My hands were clenched into fists. I wanted to say this was my shop and if I was so inclined to drag her out by her ear, I fucking would. But I didn't say that. Instead, I said, "So what makes you think he wants to speak to you now?"

Janet glared at me, then that sneer was back. "So you've got your grubby hands on it. You took control of his money, didn't you?"

"Absolutely not," I said, trying to keep my cool. "Justin has full control of all his finances."

"Stop fighting," Juss whispered.

That stopped me cold, and I looked him over. He was pale and his eyelids were heavy. "Sorry, Juss," I mumbled, taking his arm. "You need to lie down. And to take some meds. I'm sorry, baby. Let's get you upstairs."

"Jussy," Janet began, but not out of concern. God, this woman was the worst.

"The money is for me," Juss said quietly. "To pay for a nursing home or a care place in twenty years when the brain damage gets worse, so Dallas doesn't have to look after me anymore."

I stared at him; my heart dropped to my feet. "What? Justin, no. I told you that won't happen. Doctor Chang said this morning—"

"But what if it does? There's a chance it will." He shrugged and looked so damn sad. Then he turned back to his mother, his speech slow. "I have trouble with my brain and will have medical . . . things for the rest of my life."

She paused a long moment, thinking. "So there is money . . ."

"I need to go," Juss whispered, turning to me.

"And I need to talk to you," she snapped back.

I glared at her. "You need to leave."

She shot to her feet and thumped her fist on the table. "Justin, you owe me! I raised you, you cost me—"

I stood as well and yelled over the top of her. "How dare you!"

She flinched but then raised her finger at me. "I'll have a lawyer—"

Justin got to his feet. "Get out!"

She stared, and I did too. I'd never heard Justin yell. Ever.

"I said get out," he repeated, louder this time. "Get out, get out, get out!" He screamed at her, and she took a step back. "Get out!" Justin threw his walking cane at her like a javelin. It missed her head and clanged against the wall behind her, but the message he gave was a direct hit.

Flustered and shaken, she clutched at her handbag and stammered threats of calling the cops as she scurried out the door. She was still yelling obscenities as she walked to her car, as Davo and Sparra stood, staring, open-mouthed.

But Juss . . . he was pale and sweating as he put his hand to his head and swayed on his feet. I caught him before he fell and swept him up in my arms. "I'll get you upstairs, baby."

There was no resistance in him, no reaction, no . . . anything.

I carried him up the stairs and, inside, took him straight to bed. I pulled his shoes off and drew the doona over him, and his only reaction was to put the heel of his hand to the side of his head.

Fuck his mother to hell.

I ran and got his meds and had to help him sit up to sip the water to wash the tablets down. Just like those first days in hospital, he was listless, docile. He fell back onto the mattress, rolled onto his side, curled in on himself, and slowly closed his eyes.

"Sleep, baby," I whispered, tucking the doona in around

him and kissing his head. Those meds would knock him out for a while, but I still stayed there for a few minutes watching the even rise and fall of his chest. Squish jumped up on the bed and padded over to his favourite human and snuggled into Juss' side.

Then I remembered Justin's mother and wondered if she'd left yet. I hoped she hadn't, so I could go vent my rage at her. Leaving Juss asleep, I went back down to the shop to find her, unfortunately, gone.

Davo and Sparra came straight over. "Is he okay?" Sparra asked. "Saw you carryin' him upstairs. He didn't look too good."

I shook my head. I had too many emotions coursing through me right then to speak.

"What the fuck was her problem?" Davo said. "Soon as she got here, she walked in all high and mighty, asking for Jusso. I told her you weren't here, and she didn't believe me at first. I said you were both at some medical appointment but I didn't think you'd be too far away, so she just sat in the breakroom and refused to leave. Said she'd wait."

I clawed my hands, imagining them around her throat. "Ever wanted to snap someone's fucking neck?" I asked.

They both stared.

"That fucking piece of shit," I sneered. "She wants the money. She demanded he pay her, said he owes her for raising him."

"Oh, fuck that," Davo said, shaking his head.

"I wanna kick the shit out of something," I admitted, still so fucking cranky. "Juss lost his shit. He went off his head, threw his cane at her."

"We heard," Sparra said.

I shook my head. "He can't handle that kind of stress. He just fucking zoned out after, like he was those first days after the accident. I reckon the pain in his head's at a ten right now."

"Did he take his pills?" Davo asked.

I nodded, finally taking in a deep breath and calmed down a notch. "He'll be out for a while. But it's not good."

Sparra patted my shoulder. "You feeling all right?"

I nodded, then shook my head. "Dunno how I feel. Like I wanna strangle his mother. She read the newspaper article, about him getting some money. Which he thinks he needs to put aside for twenty years' time when his brain damage gets worse and he needs to go into a nursing home."

"What?" Davo asked.

I shook my head and waved my hand. "Nothing. He read some medical research piece about people who have a brain injury and what happens to them later in life. He's been stressed about that. And then she turns up. Of all people, on all the days. The piece-of-shit mother who disowned him and called him . . . horrible things."

"Well, fuck her," Davo said. "I hope she comes back. She won't get near him next time, I promise ya."

Sparra made a face. "Well, she won't be coming back for a few days. Not in that car."

"Why not?" Davo asked.

"She's gonna have two flat tyres in the next twelve or so hours." He shrugged. "She'll be fine getting home, but when she goes out to get in her car tomorrow morning, she'll have a little surprise. She really should check her valve stems more often."

Davo's mouth fell open. "You didn't? When she started yellin' and you disappeared? That's where you went?"

He sighed. "Of course not."

*Of course, yes.*

I should have reprimanded him, but all I could do was laugh. A stressed, relieved, teary laugh.

Sparra grinned. "And they were perfectly inflated when she left here, and there were no embedded nails or punctures. They'll just slowly go down over the next day or so. She can't say shit."

I let out a sigh and scrubbed a hand over my face. "I still can't believe the hide of that woman."

"She was ranting about calling the cops when she left," Davo said. "Do you reckon she will?"

I shrugged. "And tell them what?"

"That Jusso threw his cane at her."

"It didn't hit her, as much as I wish it did," I replied. "But I hope she does call the cops. They'll love to hear how she kicked him out, called him a bunch of names, and the only time she made any effort to see him was to demand money. After he's had an accident that fucked up his entire life." God, it just made me so fucking angry. "I hope she does. I'd love to see her one more time."

"God, then you *would* end up in jail," Davo said.

"And you wouldn't be able to see Jusso," Sparra added. "So, no homicide, thanks."

I sighed again, long and loud. "Yeah, I better just go up and check on him," I said. "Then I'll come straight back down. We've got three jobs in today, right?"

Davo gave me a nod. "Just do what you can do, mate. Don't stress, we'll get it done."

Of course, just then the phone rang and Davo took the cordless out of his pocket. It was another booking for later in the week, and he walked off toward the office with the phone to his ear. Sparra gave me a kind, sympathetic smile. "Go and check on him," he said.

I didn't need telling twice. I took the stairs two at a time and went inside. Juss and Squish hadn't moved at all. Though Squish opened one eye at my arrival, Justin never even stirred. His breathing was deep and even, and I didn't dare wake him. He needed to sleep, to give his brain some recovery time.

I set a bottle of water on his bedside and went back to work. I checked on him again every hour, but he slept. He'd changed positions, rolled over and upset the cat, but he never woke.

By four o'clock we'd signed off on all three jobs, and Justin still hadn't woken up. I was doing my best not to worry, but that was going about as well as could be expected.

"We've got two Suzukis in tomorrow and an ATV, first thing," I said as we were finishing up. "I don't reckon Justin will be working, but I should be."

Davo gave me a nod. "Just go, Dall. We'll lock up."

"You sure?"

Sparra nodded. "We're done here anyway. See ya in the mornin'. Tell Jusso I hope he's feeling better."

"I will. Thanks, guys."

I heard the roller door going down as I climbed the stairs, more thankful for those two guys with each step. And I'd tell them that tomorrow. But I just needed Juss to be okay first. He was still in bed, though his eyes were open.

He was on his side facing the middle of the bed, so I lay down beside him, with my head on the pillow. "Hey," I whispered.

He slow blinked, expressionless. It took him a long moment to speak and when he did, his voice was quiet and slow. "Tired."

"It's okay, baby. You can sleep."

He sighed and closed his eyes and, just like that, was

back in the land of nod. He'd had a shit day, stressed to the max, a blinding headache, and the pills he took usually put him on his arse, so I didn't mind. If he needed to sleep, then I wouldn't argue.

At least he'd been awake momentarily, and he'd spoken. That was good enough for me.

But then he slept all night through and he didn't cling to me like he usually did. He just stayed on his side, curled up, sound asleep. And in the morning, I could barely rouse him. He was sluggish and cranky like he was every morning, but it just didn't feel right. If he needed to rest all day, I wouldn't mind, but something wasn't right.

I got him out of bed and helped him to the couch and he just curled up there instead. I made him his decaf coffee and a piece of toast, knelt in front of him.

"Take a bite for me?" I asked. "I made coffee, but did you want a juice instead?"

He didn't reply, just closed his eyes. So I put the blanket over him and left his breakfast in front of him on the coffee table and went for a quick shower. When I came back out, he hadn't moved. But his eyes were half-open, though he stared into space.

I knelt in front of him again. "Juss, can you look at me?"

His eye movement was slow, but he did look at me. All that stared back at me was a familiar blankness. His right eyelid drooped a little.

My stomach felt queasy. A cold shiver ran down my scalp and all the way down my spine.

This wasn't good. Something was wrong. Sure, in the past if he'd had a big day, it took him a day to recover, but this felt . . . like something else. Something much worse.

Like all Justin's progress, his recovery, every step forward he'd taken was gone.

"Juss, can you open your mouth for me? Show me your teeth," I said, trying to remember what to ask to check for a stroke. "Juss?"

Nothing. He was just blank.

I didn't know what to do. I wasn't trained to deal with this or to know how to react. So I called the only person who I knew would be able to help. It was early, I knew I'd only get a message bank, but they'd get back to me as soon as possible.

"Uh, yeah, hi, Doctor Chang, it's Dallas Muller. Boyfriend of Justin Keith. Something's wrong with him, and I don't know what to do. If you could call me . . ."

Then it occurred to me, mid-sentence, like I was an idiot. *What the fuck are you doing, Dallas? Get him to hospital.*

"You know what? I'm gonna call him an ambulance. We'll be at John Hunter."

I ended the call, and sitting on my haunches in front of him, I called ooo. I explained that he'd had a brain injury three months ago and he'd had a stress meltdown yesterday and he'd been sleeping, but now he was mostly awake but unresponsive.

Even as I said all this, Justin simply stared into space. Like my Juss was gone all over again.

I fought tears as I spoke, giving directions and explaining that we lived above the mechanic's workshop. Leaving Juss, I raced downstairs and unlocked the front gate while I stayed on the line until I heard the sound of sirens. I ended the call and waved the ambulance in.

"He's upstairs," I said before the guy was all the way out of his seat.

They both followed me up, and Juss hadn't moved a muscle. He didn't even blink when two strangers stood in front of him. The guy knelt and asked him questions, but Juss didn't reply.

That's when the panic really started to kick in.

They asked me information about his injuries, his operations, and I tried to tell them everything. I explained that he'd been doing so well, getting back to work, and how his doctor wanted to move his appointments to fortnights instead of weekly. But then how his mother turned up yesterday and caused a scene and how he couldn't cope with stress anymore.

"He zoned out on me after she left, and his head hurt. He took his pills and went to sleep. I thought he'd wake up okay today," I told them, going to the cabinet above the fridge where we kept his meds. I took the bottle and handed it to the medic. "I thought he just needed some sleep. He said his head hurt and he put his hand to his scar. Christ, what if he's had another bleed? I should have got him to hospital yesterday."

"It's okay. We'll get him there now," the second paramedic said, her voice calm. They discussed a few things between themselves; then they mentioned the stairs.

"I can carry him down," I said. "I've done it before." I just needed him to get to hospital. I needed them to get him there now.

Maybe they were about to argue but I went to Juss and scooped him up, blanket and all. "Come on, baby. We need to get you downstairs."

I had to shuffle him a bit to get a good centre of gravity but gave the paramedic a nod before carrying him down. They hurried to get the gurney and we had him loaded into the back of the ambulance just as Davo pulled into the yard.

Fuck.

He pulled up and got out, wide-eyed. "What the hell happened?"

"It's just precautionary," the paramedic said before I could answer.

"He didn't get any better," I said. "I'll call you when I know something. If you could . . ."

"Yeah, mate, don't worry about the shop. We got it. You just go with him."

I nodded and climbed into the back of the ambulance where the other paramedic was tending to Juss. The guy shut the door, and I was holding it together okay until they flicked the sirens on. Then shit started to get really fucking real.

When we arrived at the A&E, everything was a blur. So much happened, so many people, so many questions, so fast my head spun. Until they wheeled Juss away and I was sat in a chair and told to wait. Then everything stopped.

The silence, the isolation. It was dizzying.

It was déjà vu, all over again. These white walls, the foul smell of disinfectant and sickness, the way no one made eye contact. I hated it. I hated being here; I hated that he was here again; I hated that he was going through this again.

I hated that his mother had turned up uninvited, and I hated that maybe me yelling at her stressed him out more than her yelling. That maybe I'd done this to him . . .

I should have known better.

I should have protected him and never raised my voice at her. I should have put him first instead of my temper.

As soon as Doctor Chang walked in, as soon as I saw her familiar face etched with concern and sadness, I burst into tears.

CHAPTER EIGHT

DOCTOR CHANG SAT beside me and put her arm around my shoulder. "He's had scans and blood tests," she said. "And there's nothing abnormal. There's no bleed or clot, no swelling, no new shadows. No abscess or infection. There's no change to his previous scans."

I wiped my face. "That's good, right?"

She nodded. "Yes. But . . ."

"But what?"

"There is reduced thickness in the right prefrontal cortex and left superior temporal gyrus, some enlarged amygdala volumes, and reduced caudate volumes."

"What does that mean?" I shook my head. She'd lost me after *reduced thickness*.

"Extreme stress."

"Oh God." I felt like I was gonna puke.

"Tell me what happened."

I tried to think . . . *Start at the beginning, Dallas.*

"We left your office and went out for a late breakfast. He was fine. Happy, even. He was tired; he gets tired if we go out. But he was happy. He was keen to get home. We were waiting on formal test results from the sex health clinic and he wanted to go home because the mailman would have been . . ." God, that seems like a lifetime ago. "But his mother turned up. Last time he remembers seeing her was before he moved to Darwin. She told him he was disgusting and how being gay was the worst thing he could have done to her." I took a shaky breath. "She told both of us that when we went to see her like four years ago, but Juss doesn't remember that. Probably just as well."

"So she just turned up?"

I nodded. "She read the interview in the *Times*."

She nodded slowly. "The money."

I put my hand to my forehead. "She's a horrible person. She demanded money, and I yelled at her. She yelled back at me, and I yelled some more. Then Juss yelled." I met her eyes and shook my head. "Doc, I've never heard him yell. Not ever. Not in all the years I've known him. I mean, he'd yell at the footy but never at a person. But he yelled at her and he threw his walking cane at her, and then he just shut down. He went all floppy and I carried him upstairs. I thought he just needed to sleep, ya know? When he gets too tired, he's wiped out, so I thought he just needed sleep. He said his head hurt. I got his pills for him. Just his normal ones, nothing different. He only took what he normally takes. He crashed out for hours, and I thought he needed it. He woke up a bit when I went to bed, mumbled a few words, that kind of thing. And I just thought he'd be okay this morning. But God, he couldn't even speak." Fresh tears welled in my eyes. "Christ, Doc, what did I do wrong?"

"Nothing," she said. "The yelling wasn't ideal."

"I asked her to leave and she refused. I should have picked her up and tossed her on her arse." I swallowed back more tears and anger and guilt. "I defended him. But I should have protected him. I should have *made* her leave."

"You're not responsible for her behaviour."

*No, but I'm responsible for mine. And I'm responsible for him.*

There was no point in saying that. We both knew it. Instead, I said, "How is he?" Then something horrifying occurred to me. "Oh God. Will he have lost his memory again?"

She shook her head. "It's not *im*possible, but it's not likely. The hippocampus in the scans wasn't changed."

"Oh, thank God," I breathed. Not for me . . . but Juss wouldn't cope with more memory loss.

"He'll be here overnight, at least," she continued. "They've given him something to make him sleep, to get his brain activity back to normal. And something to get his blood pressure down. Doctor Anderson's looking after him so he's in the best care. He'll fill you in on the details."

"Can I see him? I need to see him."

"I asked the nurse to come get you once he's settled."

"Thank you."

She gave me a small smile. "I assumed you'd want to see him."

I nodded, so relieved. My breath caught and it was difficult to swallow. "I was so scared."

She patted my knee. "You did the right thing. Bringing him here was the right thing to do."

"He was like those first few days after the accident. Like a zombie. Catatonic."

"Stress affects everyone differently. For someone without a brain injury, like you or me, there're many cognitive functions that allow us to cope. But for people with a brain injury, their cognitive pathways have almost certainly been disrupted and there's an overload, like a roadblock that leads to a traffic jam. The way Justin's brain processes and deals with stressful situations is very different now. Moving forward, we'll have to identify the triggers and warning signs so we can eliminate risks."

I nodded. Believe me, this was never gonna happen again. "He's gonna be pissed that his recovery took a hit. He was so happy that things were going good. I kept thinking we'd been so lucky . . ."

"You still have been," Doctor Chang said. "Even after this, he's still luckier than a lot of others."

I sighed. "I know. Sorry."

She gave me a smile. "I better go finish my rounds. Can't have other patients getting jealous," she joked. "I'll see you both again before Justin's discharged. I'd say the nurse won't be long. She knows you're here."

"Thank you."

I sighed once she'd gone and thumbed out a quick message to Davo.

*Justin's okay. He's staying tonight at least. Haven't seen him yet. I'll be back at the shop when they kick me out at lunchtime.*

I checked my watch. Lunchtime was soon anyway. I just hoped they let me see him before then . . .

And just a few minutes later, a familiar nurse, Rasida, came out to find me. "Hello, stranger. Thought we said no returns."

I stood up and tried to smile for her.

"Come on through. You've got about forty minutes before we close the ward."

We began to walk down all-too-familiar corridors. "Is he asleep?"

"Yep. He needs to be right now, so that's a good thing. We're monitoring him, though."

She stopped at a doorway and nodded to the bed inside.

This again: the cold rooms, darkened and much too quiet.

It would never get easier. And it would rip my heart to pieces every time.

Justin, in a hospital bed.

*Please let him be okay.*

It was such an odd sensation. I couldn't get my feet to work and I wanted to run to him at the same time. Needing to see him but afraid of what I might find.

But there he was. There were no bandages this time, though he was hooked up to the IV, and he had his monitor pads on his head and down his shirt. His face wasn't swollen and no bones were broken, but he looked so small. So fragile.

I pulled the uncomfortable plastic chair over to the bedside and took his hand. "Hey, baby," I whispered, fighting tears. "I'm here."

This was all so familiar, like a reoccurring nightmare. We'd been here before; we'd travelled this horrible road.

Yet it was different this time.

This wasn't just going back to square one and starting over. This was a different game. The rules had changed, and what had become our new normal would now be different again. But I didn't care. If we had to go back to square one every three or four months, I would.

I held his hand in both of mine. "The doc said you need to sleep," I whispered. "You just do what you need to do, and I'll be here when you wake up."

The first of my tears fell, and then another and another. I held the back of his hand to my cheek and cried.

GOING BACK into the workshop without Juss was strange. I'd picked up some lunch for the guys, and both Davo and Sparra stopped what they were doing when I got out of the taxi.

Davo took one look at me and his face fell. "Oh fuck."

"They said he should be okay," I said.

Davo nodded at me. "But what about you? You look like hell."

I refused to fucking cry. I shook my head and breathed in deep. "I brought us some lunch. Sorry for dropping everything onto you guys again."

Sparra clapped my shoulder. "'S all good, mate. Come on, let's eat and you can tell us how he is."

Well, I tried to eat something but didn't really have the stomach for it, and there wasn't a great deal I could tell them. Stress from his mother turning up, stress from the yelling and fighting, had basically shut his brain down. He was still asleep when I left, and Doctor Anderson, the head neurosurgeon, said his scans were okay, but we wouldn't know how long he'd be like that until he woke up.

"He was like a zombie this morning," I said, pushing my mostly uneaten lunch away.

"From stress?" Davo asked.

I nodded. "Yep. His other doc said Juss' brain is a bit like a roadmap and stress puts up roadblocks everywhere, and messages can't get through. He just . . . short-circuited."

"So no more stress," Sparra said with a hard nod.

"No, no more stress."

"When can he come home?" Davo asked.

"Hopefully tomorrow. We have to see how he is when

he wakes up first. If he still can't speak or hear commands, then I don't know . . ."

Davo's eyes went wide. "Can't speak?"

"Yeah. It wasn't good."

He frowned. "Fucking hell."

I took a deep breath. "I've got about two and a half hours before they'll let me back in to see him, and I need to keep busy. So tell me what needs doing, and I'll do it."

Two and a half hours of working my arse off was exactly what I needed, and having another set of hands to help was exactly what Davo and Sparra needed. Between the three of us we got almost all of it done, and I felt better about leaving for the afternoon knowing I'd helped out some.

I'd still be lost without those two guys, Davo especially. And knowing he'd be needing time away at some point with his new baby on the way made me more determined to do the right thing by him.

I needed to do something to make the shop run more efficiently in the times I couldn't be there. I just needed to put it away for the minute and concentrate on Juss, and once he was home and on the mend, I could start putting together a plan to make all our lives easier.

JUSS WAS STILL ASLEEP when I got back to the hospital, though the nurse said he'd been stirring. I took my seat beside his bed and took his hand. "Hey, baby," I whispered. "I'm here."

He was utterly motionless, except for the slow and steady rise and fall of his chest. After a few minutes, his fingers flinched in mine and his eyelids fluttered before he startled awake. His eyes opened and he stared at the ceiling for a long moment before he slowly turned his head to look at me.

His face was without expression; his eyes held no emotion.

He stared at me like he had when he first woke up after his accident and didn't remember who I was.

He stared at me like I was a stranger, all over again.

No.

*No, no no no no.*

*Please God, no.*

My heart squeezed to the point of pain, and fear sent ice through my veins.

This wasn't happening. Not again. He wouldn't survive going through this again, and I wasn't sure I would either.

"Juss? You're okay. You're in the hospital," I whispered, my voice cracking.

He stared, then he slow blinked, his gaze blank and distant. My whole chest burned and ached, and I fought tears.

Then something clicked in his brain, I could see it in his eyes. His gaze locked onto mine and the corner of his lip picked up. "Dallas," he breathed.

And the weight of relief crushed me. I sagged, put his hand to my cheek, and sobbed.

# CHAPTER NINE

THE DOCTORS DID their thing with Juss and I stood aside to get out of their way. He was okay, and that was all that mattered to me. He remembered me, and he spoke. He even smiled.

He was still totally wiped and slow blinked a lot, but he was going to be okay.

Even still, he was definitely staying in overnight and they'd be back to see how he was in the morning, and then it was just me and him again.

I went back to my side of his bed and pulled the seat over. "Hey, you," I murmured.

"Hey." He smiled, exhausted.

"How do you feel? Can I get you anything? Water?"

He lifted his hand as though it weighed a tonne. "You can hold my hand."

I was quick to take it, threading our fingers. I kissed his knuckles, his palm. "You scared me, baby. I was so worried."

"Sorry. Didn't mean to."

"I know. I'm just glad you're okay."

"So tired."

"You gotta stay here tonight," I said, frowning. As much as I hated it, if the docs said he needed to be here, then he needed to be here. "I'm sure they'll look after you just fine."

He slow blinked. "Stay for as long as you can."

That made me smile. "Baby, I wouldn't be anywhere else."

He dozed some more, and I sat there watching the rise and fall of his chest, watching the lines on the machines and listening to all the beeps, like it was some kind of orchestra. Time dragged, but at least it gave me some time to do some research on my phone.

I needed to get my shit together at the shop. I couldn't do everything. I couldn't be there all the time. And sure, the money stranglehold was lessened with the insurance approval, but if I wasn't careful, I'd find myself right back in trouble.

I needed to work smarter, not harder. And I had a good idea of where to start, too.

"You're cute when you're thinking," Juss whispered.

I looked up to find him, obviously, awake. I put my phone down. "Hey. Sorry, I was just reading . . . How are you feeling?"

"'Kay. Thirsty."

I held a cup of water to his lips and he took a few sips before sagging back onto the mattress. "Thanks."

"How's your headache?"

"'S okay. Wish I was at home."

"Me too. Tomorrow, hopefully."

"Yeah."

"I'm supposed to work tomorrow," he mumbled.

"It's okay, Juss. I know the boss."

He smiled again, though his eyes closed. He lifted his

hand again even though he was almost asleep. "Hold, please."

This time I took his hand in both of mine and held onto it until they made me leave at dinner time.

———

THE NEXT MORNING, Juss was sitting up in the hospital bed. He was picking at food on his breakfast tray and his whole face lit up when he saw me. "Oh, hey."

"Good morning," I said, putting a bag on my seat. I leaned in and gave him a kiss. "You're looking much brighter today."

"Feel better. Still not great, and I reckon I'll need to be the king of naps today, but I do feel better."

"The king of naps," I repeated. "I like that."

He pushed his table tray away. "The food here is still bad."

I pulled his favourite brand of decaf iced coffee out of the bag. "Thought you might want one of these."

His smile turned into something sweet and gushy. "Oh my God. Dall . . ."

I handed it over with a kiss to his cheek. "Anything for my king of naps."

Doctor Anderson came by mid-morning, and after going over his file and having a bit of a chat with us, he declared Justin a free man. His recovery from yesterday to today might seem remarkable, like he was almost back to normal, but the doc reassured us that wasn't the case.

We just had to promise to take it easy for a week, and absolutely no stress. Justin readily agreed, not just to get parole from hospital, but because he genuinely had no intention of getting off the couch.

He was beat.

This whole ordeal had knocked him on his arse and was a stark reminder that we needed to take his health seriously. Because we learned the hard and fast way that it could all go very bad, very quickly.

We were still waiting for the final discharge papers when Doctor Chang stuck her head in. "Someone's looking better today." Then she looked at me. "Actually, make that two someones looking a lot better than they were yesterday."

"Morning," I said with a smile.

She walked into where Juss was sitting on the bed, dressed and ready to go home. "I have some good news for you, Justin."

"I never have to come back?" he asked, hopeful.

She chuckled. "You don't need to have your scheduled scans next week like we talked about, because you had them all yesterday."

"Does he still have to come in for an appointment then?" I asked.

"Yep. You both can't get away from me that easily," she said with a wink. "I know we talked about moving to fortnightly appointments, but we might need to hold off on that for another week or so. We can start focusing on some coping techniques for stress."

"Doctor Anderson already did that," Juss said.

"Yep, and we'll be going over it again," she said brightly. He wasn't getting out of it, obviously.

"I know how to start," Juss said. "Never see my mother again. That's it. Step one and only."

Doctor Chang frowned, but I agreed with Juss. "She's not welcome at our place ever again."

"Well," she said. "At least we know where to start."

I went to Juss and rubbed his back, kissing the side of his head. "If and when you ever decide to see her again, it'll be on your terms. Not hers, okay?"

He nodded and looked up at me, giving me a small smile. "I'm so tired, babe."

I pulled him against me and held him, which was kind of awkward since he was sitting on the bed. But he didn't mind, because he sighed and relaxed in my arms. "We'll be home soon," I whispered, rubbing his back.

Doctor Chang studied Juss for a moment and mouthed, "I think he's asleep." Smiling, she pointed to the door. "See you next week."

I didn't dare move, even long after she'd gone because, yeah, Juss had fallen asleep against me. He was kind of side-on but his neck was well supported, so I left him right where he was. He woke up when the nurse brought his discharge papers, and he didn't even argue about the wheel-chair he had to use to leave. That's how exhausted he was.

He slept on the way home and barely stirred when I woke him up to get him out of the ute. I helped him up the stairs and he walked himself straight back to bed. He was out like a light, so I put everything he might need on his bedside table and went downstairs.

Of course, Davo and Sparra had stopped what they were doing. "How is he?" Davo asked.

"He's okay. Tired as hell, probably will be for a while. I doubt he'll be down here working this week, but we'll see."

"Fair enough," Sparra said.

I ran my hands through my hair and sighed. "You two got a second? I wanna run something past ya's before I start making phone calls."

Davo nodded. "I could always have a coffee."

With three fresh brews, we sat at the breakroom table

and they waited for me to start talking. "It's been a shit few months, and I know my time has been split between here and everything else. That's not fair on you guys, and I just want you to know that I really do appreciate it." They were both about to argue or say something to downplay my thanks. I put my hand up. "I mean it. And anyway, I've been thinking of something I could do to make things run easier and smoother for you two. And for the business, but mostly for you two. I think yesterday proved to me that I can't always be here. Juss' health has to be a priority. I mean, this place and you guys are a priority too. So I can't do all this on my own. I can't manage this and you guys and Juss and emergencies and whatnot. So I was thinking I needed help."

"What kind of help, Dallas?" Davo asked.

"I don't want to hire another mechanic. I love our little team and I don't want to replace Justin because his station will be his until he's ready to come back to it. And I don't want to spend every minute of every day in the office because that's not what I love doing. I wanna be working on bikes. It's what we do, right?"

Sparra nodded. "Yep."

"So I was thinking I might hire an office manager. Someone to take care of the phones, the bookings, the orders, the . . . everything that I've been slacking on, basically. Everything that Davo's pretty much been doing in my absence. So," I said, looking right at him. "Davo, first choice is yours. If you want to be the office manager here, the job's yours."

He shot me a stunned look. "Like, in your office and not out there working on bikes and stuff?"

"Well, yeah."

He made a face. "Um, well, thanks for the offer, and I

don't mind helping out when you need it, but Dallas, I wanna be working on bikes too. It's what we do, right?"

Sparra put his hands up in surrender. "Jesus, don't look at me next. I don't want it."

I sighed with relief. "Oh, thank fuck," I said with a laugh. "I mean, I had to offer it to ya, but damn, I'd be well and truly screwed trying to replace either of you guys on the floor."

Davo smiled. "So you're gonna put someone on the phones? Can't say I'm sad about that."

"Yeah, I know. Me either. I should've done it years ago. When I first started, I just did it all. Then you guys came along and helped out on the floor so I could do more stuff in the office, and that was great, but it was never my strong point. It's just not me. I love my business, and I certainly don't want to lose it, so I should start running it like . . . well, a business."

I sipped my coffee, ignoring the lack of sleep from last night. "That'll let you guys do your jobs with no interruptions, and it will let me do mine. I can be on the floor when I need to be, or I can go to doctor appointments without worrying that you guys are left with everything. And all things going well, it means we can book in more jobs because we're not stopping every five minutes to answer phones and take bookings or chase parts or orders."

"Sounds good," Davo said. "But Dallas, you know we don't mind, right?"

"I know, but I do. I put too much on you both. Oh," I added. "I've got the rep for those hoists coming by next week."

Sparra clapped his hands together and grinned. "We gonna be fancy!"

I laughed and let out a long breath. "Well, enough of the

bullshit. I'm gonna go call an employment place and get the ball rolling then I can help both of you on the bikes."

---

"HEY, BEAUTIFUL," I said, kissing Juss' forehead. He was on the couch when I finally called it a day and went upstairs. He was dozy and had slept on and off all day, but he smiled.

"Hey."

I slumped onto the couch beside him and put my head on his lap. I looked up at him. "I was thinking omelettes for dinner."

His fingers found my hair and he was still smiling at me. "Sounds good."

Well, I wasn't sure about good. But they were quick and easy and required minimal effort to eat with no loud crunching or heavy chewing for Juss.

"But I could just lie here for a bit first," I said. "And you could keep running your fingers through my hair."

He chuckled. "I could." He put one hand to work on my hair but his other hand sat on my chest, and I took that hand in mine, holding it tight. There was some surfing championship on the TV, the volume and brightness were low, but it was relaxing to watch. "This is nice," he whispered.

"Being here with you like this is the best."

He hummed and played with my hair for a bit. "How was work?" His question was slow, so he was still tired, but he wasn't nodding off.

"Yeah, we got it all done," I said. "I'm gonna hire someone for the office, Juss. Someone to answer the phones and organise the booking sheets and do some paperwork and ordering for me. That way I can get more work done in the shop."

His hand stilled in my hair. "Is that because of me?"

"Not at all, baby. It's long overdue, and having to stop halfway through a job to take a phone call is a pain for everyone. I want you and me and Davo and Sparra to be able to get our work done. Especially if you and I are away, then poor Davo is trying to do too much."

Juss nodded and took some time to think about all that. "Sorry I can't do more."

"Don't be sorry, Juss. It is what it is. You need to rest first, then you can worry about that. You'll be back to work soon enough. Oh," I said, remembering just now. "I've got a guy coming next week to see which hoist systems we want. That's kinda exciting, and also long overdue. I should have done that years ago. And we'll get those roller chairs that go with them, and Sparra already wants to race you on your scooter. From one end of the shop to the other."

Juss eventually smiled. "I'll beat him."

I snorted as I got up. "You will." I kissed the side of his head on my way to the kitchen, and ten minutes later, we were eating ham, cheese, and capsicum omelettes. And ten minutes after dinner, Juss was ready for bed again.

Even though it was kind of early, I really hadn't slept much the night before, so I got ready for bed with him. We settled in under the covers and Juss automatically found his spot, snuggled into me. "My wing tattoo pillow," he mumbled.

I wrapped him up tight, his familiar body, his familiar warmth was like a balm. "God, I missed you last night. Squish missed you too."

"Don't ever want to go back to hospital," he murmured.

"I know, baby."

"Was so scared."

"Me too."

"Don't want to be like that again." Maybe it was easier for him to admit these things in the dark.

I rubbed his back. "I promise I'll protect you, baby. I won't let it get to that ever again."

He nodded against my chest and sighed as he relaxed into a deep sleep. I revelled in the fact he was in my arms again, safe and well, where I wanted to keep him forever.

# CHAPTER TEN

JUSS DIDN'T COME DOWNSTAIRS the next two days. He was still wiped, but mostly happy, and spent his time dozing on the couch or in bed. On day three, he came down for a little while in the morning to see the boys. He tidied up a few things here and there, but it was mostly just to be social, to have a laugh, and to feel the warmth of the sun on his skin. He made dinner that night and did some laundry, so he was definitely feeling better.

He was still clingy, though, not that I minded that part. But as soon as he saw me, he needed touch: a hug, a kiss, cuddling on the couch. He'd admitted that his setback had scared him, and I believed him.

He didn't complain about being bored, about being cooped up inside, about not being able to work. I think what scared him most was how close he'd come to going that one step too far, one step from not being able to return.

He was truly listening to his body, not pushing to get back to his new normal, but rather letting his mind and body tell him when he was ready.

On Friday, Juss stayed downstairs with us for a little bit

longer, though it was probably just out of curiosity. I was expecting three people to come in for an interview before lunch. The employment agency had done the hard work and narrowed down a prospective employee, but I would get to meet and decide who I thought would be the best fit.

The first girl was young and probably had potential but couldn't even get through the interview without checking her phone. The second was a guy who Davo and I had caught checking out Justin, and when he realised he'd been caught, he just grinned and mumbled something about a snack.

He was obviously a hard fucking no.

I went through with the interview with him, though I'd already made up my mind. It didn't help the fact that Davo stood where I could see him through the doorway of my office, laughing his damn head off.

When he'd gone, Davo, still grinning, said, "Your face. The whole interview. Oh my God, so funny."

"What was funny?" Juss asked.

"That guy thought you were a snack," Davo said, laughing again. "Thought Dallas was gonna kill him."

Justin looked confused and horrified. "A snack?"

"Something to eat," Sparra explained. "It's a new thing the kids say these days."

It took him a second, but he nodded. "Oh."

I grumbled. "He didn't even try to hide it." I pointed to my chest. "Justin's *my* snack. And anyway, he didn't know jack shit about bikes or nothing—"

I stopped talking because Davo was laughing so hard he was gonna bust something. He grabbed his side. "Ow, fuck. A stitch."

Served him right.

Juss was smiling at me. "I'm your snack, am I?"

I was pouting, and I didn't care. "Yes."

That, of course, set Davo off laughing again, though he still had to hold his side. Didn't stop him. "Oh God, jealous Dallas is my favourite."

Fucker.

Justin came into my office, around to my chair, and leaned his arse against my desk. It was good to see him smile. "Jealous Dallas is my favourite too."

I looked up at him and couldn't help but laugh, shaking my head at myself. "Sorry. You're not *my* snack. I shouldn't have said that."

He met my gaze. "Yes I am."

I laughed and pulled out my wallet, giving Juss my credit card. "Speaking of snacks. Can you please put in a lunch order from the takeaway shop down the road and have it delivered? Get the fellas what they want." I looked out the door. "Dunno why I'm feeding Davo."

Davo just laughed from around the corner. "I take it back. Lunch-buying Dallas is my favourite."

Juss took the card and leaned down and gave me a smiley kiss. He limped out of my office and went and sat in the breakroom, and I heard him and Sparra discussing lunch. I thought Sparra might do the ordering over the phone, but no, Juss did it. He was tired and I knew, after lunch, he'd be sleeping for a while.

Davo appeared at my door, trying to look serious. "Someone here to see you, boss."

It was my next, and final, interview, and I was beginning to lose hope. But in walked a woman with short black hair, maybe in her 40s, and she had an easy smile. She held out her hand for me to shake and nodded to where Juss' bike stood in the corner. "Nice. Is that a 2016 or '17?"

She knew bikes.

"Ah, 2016. You like KTMs?"

"My two sons ride," she said. "And my husband, but mostly the boys. Spent a lot of weekends at racetracks when they were growing up."

I grinned at her. "Come into my office," I said, but I already knew.

Her name was Toni and she was a straight-shooter, no-nonsense woman who knew her way around accounting programs and stocktakes like she knew which KTM she was looking at by just a glance.

I liked her, and she was a perfect fit for us.

She had no problem dealing with four guys. She lived with three: her husband and two grown sons. She knew how to catalogue and order parts. She'd worked the last six years at an auto-supply shop but left when the business sold. She had no problem whatsoever with the fact that two out of the four guys working here were gay and that we were actually a couple. She just wouldn't pick sides if we had a fight, because her usual advice that the guy was always wrong wouldn't do us much good.

I had to make it official with the employment agency, but I was certain we'd found our newest team member.

And if I'd felt any apprehension at all, it was gone. Now I just felt . . . relieved.

Toni left and lunch arrived, and the mood around the lunch table was relaxed and happy. Though Juss was smiling as he ate, he could barely keep his eyes open. "I think I'm done," he said slowly, pushing his half-eaten burger away. "It's nap o'clock for me."

I helped him up the stairs, and again, he went to bed and not to the sofa. He was so tired, and with some warm food in his belly, he fell straight to sleep.

I put his boots by the bed, and when I slid his phone

onto the bedside table, it vibrated so I naturally looked at the screen.

He'd had five missed calls and three missed messages.

I didn't know the number or look who the messages were from or what they said. I didn't want to intrude on his privacy like that. If he'd missed a medical call, they'd call me, so it wasn't urgent. And if Becca couldn't get through to him, she'd call me as well.

The only person I could think of, and the reason he hadn't answered the calls or taken the messages, would be his mother.

So help me God, if that woman . . .

Then I remembered that my temper had contributed to Juss' stress overload so I took a deep breath and counted to ten. I had to get a handle on that shit from now on.

I left Squish in charge of sleeping supervision and went back downstairs. We had to hook in and get our jobs finished, but the last customer left at knock-off time and we finished the week on a good note. I helped the customer load the bike onto his trailer while Davo and Sparra finished up in the shop. When I came back in, Juss was there helping them.

He looked like he'd just woken up, which meant he must have slept for about four hours. "Hey," I said.

He shoved his hands into his hoodie pockets and smiled. "Hey. Just wanted to see the fellas before they left. Let 'em know I'll be back to work on Monday."

"You feel up to that?" I asked.

He gave a nod. "If I take it easy this weekend, yeah. Just small stuff, though. And if it's too much, I'll just tap out."

I grinned at him. "Sounds great. And you'll be fine. I know it." He had always been determined, but he also seemed to have a newfound respect for his limitations.

"It helps that the boss loves me and we live right upstairs," he added.

"Yes, he does."

"Hey, Jusso," Davo called out as he wheeled the toolbox into the storage room. "Gimme a hand with this."

So while they busied themselves with packing up, I went to finalise a bit more paperwork. I was filling in the weekly EPA report when Davo and Sparra called it a day, and Juss came into my office. He parked himself in his usual spot—his arse against my desk. "Just gotta get this motor oil disposal written up, then I'm all done."

"That's okay, take your time, I'll just wait right here." He was quiet for a bit while I entered in some numbers. "Will you miss this? The paperwork? The office?"

I snorted. "God, no."

"This office could use a pot plant," he said randomly.

"Uh, I guess it could." I looked around the office. It was functional but drab. It was also dusty as hell. "I might give myself one job this weekend, and that's to clean the shit out of here before Toni starts."

"Yeah, it could do with some organising. Some trays and maybe some new pens and stuff. I don't know what office people like."

I chuckled, because this was proof that Juss was feeling much better. He was having proper connective thoughts instead of the zombie he had been since his stay in hospital earlier this week.

"Oh, what's this?" he said, reaching for a pile of mail that still sat in my in-tray. Something else I was going to attack this weekend. "This one's for me." He flipped through the envelopes. "And one for you."

Oh, shit. "They came the other day. I was going to bring

them upstairs, sorry. I got busy. Um, I think they might be those test results we were waiting on."

His gaze shot to mine. "The blood tests?"

"Yep. I forgot about them, to be honest. We got a little sidetracked, didn't we?"

He hummed and studied the envelope, turning it over in his hand. Then he held it out to me. "Can you read it for me? I don't think I could handle bad news right now. If something's wrong, just say, 'Oh goodie, more dick swabbing,' and I'll understand."

Chuckling, I took the envelope. "I can read it for you." I undid the envelope and unfolded the paper. It was the lab results, and after a quick scan down the list, I handed it back. "No more dick swabbing."

And yeah, I was relieved. Not for the prospect of sex, but because he wasn't joking when he said he couldn't handle bad news right now.

"Oh, thank God," he said, reading over it. "Now do yours."

I undid mine and read over it. "No more dick swabbing for me either."

Juss grinned. "I can swab it for you if you want."

I laughed and handed him my lab results so he could see. "And just so you know, baby. This doesn't mean we have to rush into anything. It just means we can, when you're ready."

He looked up from the letter and leaned down for a kiss. "I know. But thank you for saying it."

I finished up the last of the report and shut the computer down, and making sure everything was locked up, we went upstairs. Juss suggested lamb and salad for dinner, which sounded bloody good to me, and it would take all of fifteen minutes to make. He put together the salad and I grilled the meat, and when we sat down to eat, his phone buzzed on the table.

He looked at the number and let it ring out. "Not gonna answer it?" I asked.

"No. It's my mother. Should have got a new number years ago."

"Would you like me to talk to her? I can ask her to stop calling you. Or I can just block her number for you."

He chewed a mouthful of salad, frowning as he swallowed. "I don't want it to trigger another episode."

"Oh, baby," I said, rubbing his arm. "Let's just block her number and then you don't have to deal with her at all."

He pushed his dinner around with his fork. "I just want her out of my life. She doesn't love me. She doesn't even like me. If I did give her money, it wouldn't be enough. If I gave her everything and she knew it was all gone, she'd take it and wouldn't speak to me again."

God, I hated that she hurt him so much.

"So, we'll take screenshots of her messages and of how many times she's tried to call, then we'll block her. If she becomes a problem, we let the police handle it, okay? You don't have to worry about her, if that's what you want."

He sighed and nodded. "Sounds good."

"Baby, don't stress over anything. Anything you need me to handle, I will take care of for you. If you need to talk about something to get it off your mind, talk away. Or write it down for Doctor Chang if you don't want to talk to me about it."

His gaze shot to mine. "I don't want secrets from you."

"I know. But sometimes you might want to talk to someone else. And that's okay. Or talk to Sparra. I'm sure he wouldn't mind. Or Becca. It doesn't have to be me, just talk to someone. Don't bottle anything up."

He sipped his mineral water and gave me a smile. "Okay." He ate a slice of meat. "So can we talk about the snack comment today? And jealous Dallas. Because I've never met jealous Dallas before, and I have to admit, I liked him."

I laughed. "I told you before I wasn't perfect. Jealousy is something I need to work on."

He smiled, very pleased with himself. "I've never had anyone be jealous over me before. It's kinda hot. Not sure I'm overly fond of the caveman, chest-beating thing, but hearing you say I'm yours was . . . good."

"Okay, well, first up, that guy was out of line. He came for a job interview and made inappropriate comments about another employee. Another employee who just happened to be my boyfriend, no less. He didn't know that, but that's not the point."

"True."

"And Davo just happened to be there and reckoned the look on my face was funny. But the guy totally checked you out and called you a snack. He was lucky I didn't throw him out, and it was probably just as well Davo was laughing so much or I might have."

Juss seemed to find something very amusing. "I do like jealous Dallas. Have you ever thrown someone out over me before? At a bar or a club?"

"No. Thankfully. I guess I never had to. There might have been a time or two where I had to put my arm around you to prove a point." *Or stick my tongue down your throat.* "But no one ever dared call you a snack to my face."

He chuckled at that. "Probably because you're huge and your 'he's *my* snack' face is pretty scary." Then he sighed happily. "Well, I don't find it scary. I rather like it."

"Just not the chest-thumping caveman kind."

"Right. Although, if you wanted to throw me over your shoulder and take me back to your cave, I wouldn't put up a fight. Like, at all."

That made me laugh. "I'll keep that in mind."

Juss got up from his seat and sat on my lap. I had to pull my chair out a bit so he could fit, but he just sat right down and put his arm around my shoulder, his forehead pressed to mine. "No one's ever stood up for me or got all protective of me. I like it."

I kissed him. "I will always look out for you. Even if sometimes I go overboard and yell, like I yelled at your mother. I'm sorry I did that. It stressed you out, but she wanted to hurt you and I just saw red. I should have reacted better."

Justin scratched my beard with his thumb. "I'm glad you did. And it wasn't just you yelling that stressed me out. Her coming here and demanding money, telling me I owe her . . ." He shook his head. "She stressed me out. Not you."

"But I didn't help, and I'm sorry."

He lifted my chin up and planted a soft kiss on my lips. "I forgive you. I don't forgive her."

And then, because the devil heard her name, Juss' phone rang again. He groaned at the number. "Want me to block her?" I asked.

He nodded, so I ended the call and took some screenshots of her numerous attempts to contact him, then the text messages, which were all variations of *the least you could do is answer my calls* and *how dare you*, and then, with great satisfaction, I blocked her number.

"Done."

He smiled ruefully. "Thank you. I didn't know how to do it and didn't want to press her name and accidentally dial her instead."

I put my arms around him and buried my face against his arm. It was never easy to make cutting off a family member official, and even though he'd wanted to do it, it still had to sting. "I'm sorry, baby."

"Don't be. I'm not."

I looked up at him. "Not even a little?"

He shook his head. "This is her doing, not mine. She disowned me first. Now I'm just returning the favour. And anyway, remember how you said we choose our own family?"

I nodded.

"Well, I've chosen mine." He kissed me soundly. Then he picked up my fork and stabbed some meat and brought it to my lips. "Open wide."

I laughed and he shoved the fork in my mouth. "You're gonna feed me?" I asked.

"For all the times you helped me, now it's your turn."

He continued to feed me until my plate was empty and he even had some more of his own. It was fun and cute, we laughed a lot, and it had been far too long since we'd done anything fun and cute. The fact that he punctuated every forkful with a kiss made it even better.

He put the fork down and turned his full attention to me. "You know," he said with a kiss. "I slept a lot today, so I'm not too tired."

I chuckled because I was pretty sure I knew where he was going with this. "Is that so?"

He kissed me again, a little softer, more playful. "And we did get those test results back."

I hummed, not too sure if he was up for anything rigorous. "You're supposed to be on bed rest."

He smiled. "So take me to bed."

# CHAPTER ELEVEN

I CERTAINLY WASN'T GOING to say no. I wanted Juss to feel good to replace the pain he lived with, even just for a while. He'd been getting better over the last three days, but he still wasn't anywhere near back to good.

"Are you sure?"

He nodded quickly. "I trust you."

Given he was still sitting on my lap, I picked him up as I stood, making him laugh. I carried him to our room and laid him on the bed, then climbed up his body and gently laid my weight on him.

His smile and the way he chewed on his bottom lip told me he was fine, but I had to be careful of his injuries. He spread his legs, slowly moving his right leg, and I froze. "Juss."

He held my gaze. "I want this."

God, the fierceness in his eyes was so familiar, but still so new. "We'll just take small steps, baby. We don't need to go too far. I just want to make you feel good."

He flexed his hips, grinding our erections together. "I already feel good, Dall. I want you to make me come."

I kissed him. "That I can do." I went to kiss him again, but he stopped me. I worried that I'd hurt him. "What is it?"

"We need to be naked first. Both of us. Right now."

I laughed, because that was such a Justin thing to say. I would never tire of seeing snippets of the real him.

But I obeyed and undressed him first, then myself, and crawled back under the covers with him. I moved on top of him again and he was quick to pull me in for a kiss, and we soon found a rhythm. Our cocks slid against each other and Juss rolled his hips. I grinded in an ebb and flow of desire and love.

He bent his left leg, giving me more room and making himself open for me. I could so easily push into him from this position, and he knew it. He dug his fingernails and I had to stop myself from thrusting into him. I pulled back with a laugh and sat back on my haunches.

"You remember how to push my buttons just fine," I said. Then I took in the sight before me. His legs were spread, his cock hard, his lips kiss-swollen. I went forward, pressing my palm into the mattress to keep my weight off him, my cock aching for touch. "You are so fucking hot right now."

He groaned and tried to pull me back down on him. "Dall, I need something . . . I don't know what I can handle, but I need it."

"I know what you need, baby," I murmured. "And I know exactly how you like it."

He whined and I took that as my cue. His body couldn't handle being so strung out right now.

I kissed him one more time before kissing down his body, his jaw, his neck, his collarbone, his nipples. He groaned when I sucked his nipple in between my teeth, just like he always did.

Some things never changed.

I moved down to his cock, licked up the shaft. He was leaking precome so I swiped it with my finger and rubbed it against his arsehole.

He rocked his hips. "Oh God."

I grinned as I took him into my mouth. I sucked him as I pushed a finger into him, and he welcomed it. I pumped his cock in my fist and worked more precome out of him, using it as lube to push a second finger inside him.

Juss groaned out as I stretched him and sucked him. "Dallas, I'm gonna—"

He came, his back arching and he cried out. I swallowed his orgasm and he was racked with tremors. I pulled my fingers out and worked my own cock, so close already . . . Slick with precome, I fucked my fist, spilling my seed on his belly.

I collapsed at his side, careful of his leg, and pulled the blankets up. I wrapped my arms around him, making him the little spoon, and I kissed the back of his neck. "You feel okay?"

He chuckled. "I feel so good right now. I'm a mess, but I don't care. I don't want to move."

"Good," I whispered, kissing his neck, his shoulder. "I never want to let you go."

His sigh was almost a moan. "I can feel your cock," he whispered. I was pressed right against him, my half-hard dick was against his arse. He writhed a little, trying to get me aligned. He brought his injured leg up slowly and pushed his arse back. "You could just . . ."

"Juss," I breathed.

"Just the tip, just a little bit. Let me feel it."

Fuck.

Of course, my half-hard dick twitched at the idea, and

my body moved without any conscious thought. I could have pushed into him so easily. I wanted to be buried inside him, and he wanted it as well . . .

I shifted my hips, getting a better angle, and pushed upward, into.

Just the tip, just a little . . . was never going to be enough.

I pushed my softening dick against his hole; he was still slick and ready.

"Please, Dall."

I never could bear to hear him beg.

I slid into him and he cried out, pushing his arse back and arching his back, just like he always used to. Tight and hot, he took me.

My body knew his body. My cock knew and it glided right into home. We were joined. We were as one. Like we'd done a thousand times, but brand new.

I held his back to my front as I pushed inside, feeling his breaths, his heart. He felt so, so good.

"Oh God," he whispered. "Fuck, Dallas, just stay right there."

"Am I hurting you?" I asked, kissing the back of his neck. I ran my hands up his sides and down again, gripping his hips.

"No, God no," he said, his voice tight.

I knew that sound. I knew that tremor. Fucking hell, he was going to come again.

"Dallas," he murmured, gripping the blankets before us.

I rolled my hips, thrusting. "I know, baby."

"Oh God."

And just like that, he came again.

I think he was stunned, shocked that his body was able

to do that. The truth was, I'd made him come like that a hundred times.

He loved my cock in his arse. He *loved* it. I didn't need to be fully hard or fucking him. Just having me inside him was enough to get him off.

I pulled out slowly and he whined, but I carefully rolled him over so I could hold him properly. "You feel okay?"

"I feel . . . amazing."

I snorted. "You are amazing."

"Your dick is amazing."

I laughed at that.

"You were inside me, after you finished, and you got me off," he added.

I kissed the side of his head. "I know what you like, baby."

He went to move and had to unpeel our skin. "Uh, we're stuck."

I laughed. "Shower time." I got out of bed and helped him to his feet. "How do you feel?"

"I feel good. Tired, but that's nothing new."

"How about a hot shower, toasted sandwiches for dinner, and we hit the couch for whatever's left of the footy?"

"Sounds good."

After a quick scrub clean, Juss made toasted ham and cheese sandwiches, I stripped and remade the bed, and we caught the last twenty minutes of footy. Well, I did. Juss was asleep about ten seconds in.

---

JUSTIN DID IMPROVE over the weekend. He took it easy, never pushing himself, and every day since his most recent hospital stay, he got stronger. By Monday, he was feeling pretty good. He'd spoken to his sister a few times about their mother, and Becca was totally cool with Juss' decision to cut their mother from his life. Actually, Bec was one more snide comment from cutting her out too. It wasn't as though their mother was a huge part in their lives anyway, but Bec was sick of the toxicity as well.

It had been a long time coming and helped Juss feel better about the whole thing. He adored Bec and she him, and even though she lived two hours away, her support was an important part of his overall recovery.

Not just his recovery from his stress-induced meltdown, but his recovery overall.

And so was work. After a week off, he was itching to get his hands dirty. Monday morning he came out wearing his work overalls and boots, grinning. "Hey, boss."

I chuckled into my coffee, because Juss never smiled in the morning. "Keen to get back to work?" He was only going to do a few hours, just to see how he felt.

"Keen as mustard."

I snorted and handed him his coffee. "Toast?"

"Let me make it for you," he said, sipping his coffee, then threw some bread into the toaster.

He really was in a good mood. "Thanks, baby."

He came in for a long hug while the toast cooked. "It's gonna be a good week."

"I think so too," I said. God, I hoped so. "The guys won't recognise the office." I'd spent most of the weekend cleaning and clearing shit out. Juss helped but mostly just sat on the desk and supervised.

"And Toni starts on Wednesday?" he asked as he buttered the toast.

"Yep."

He slathered on some Vegemite and handed me a piece. "And the hoist rep is coming today?"

"Yep."

He grinned. "It's gonna be a good week."

My God, it did ridiculously crazy things to my heart to see him so happy. "In case I haven't told you enough lately, I love you."

He laughed as he ate. "You have, but you can keep telling me. Love you too." He sipped his coffee, still smiling. "And because I'm feeling good, and if things stay good, you get to dick me properly."

I almost choked on my coffee. I coughed and spluttered and he patted me on the back, that cheeky grin in full effect. "The doc said a week, and you promised."

"I promised?" I didn't recall a promise.

"Yesterday, when I had your dick in my mouth, you said you couldn't wait to fuck me. I said, 'Promise?' And you said, 'Promise.'"

My mouth fell open. Okay, I think I remembered that conversation, but God help me, I would have said anything when he was teasing me with his tongue. "You can't use anything I said under duress. That's not fair."

He laughed. "You promised, Dall."

I pinched his chin and drew him in for another kiss. "You don't play fair."

He smiled as he finished his toast. "It's gonna be such a good week."

---

THE SALES REP with the hoists was a guy named Connor. He was a decent sort of bloke, a bit confident, but he knew his stuff. He brought with him two types of hoist, one standard model and one higher-end. He showed us all the bells and whistles and explained work safety and ergonomics and all that salesman spiel.

"If you've got a bike we could demonstrate with . . ." he said.

The two client bikes we had in store were both on stands, one without a tyre and one without its handlebars. Not that I would have been comfortable using a client's bike anyway.

"What about mine?" Justin said, nodding to his bike in the corner. "I'll bring it over."

Mine was behind Juss' bike but he was already off his scooter and walking to get it. I went to help him, but Sparra took my arm. "He's got it," he whispered.

I knew I had to let Justin do things on his own, but what if it fell on him?

Juss kicked the stand up and wheeled his bike over, trying not to grin too wide. "Be careful with her," he said to Connor. "I'm gonna ride her again one day, aren't I, Dall?"

Everyone turned to me. He was going to ride again one day. But not just yet. "Yep. One day. Might be a while before we tackle any motocross tracks though."

Connor showed us how to get the bike onto the hoist, secure it, demonstrating all its features. He noticed Juss get back on his scooter and fix his right leg onto the footrest, but Connor never missed a beat. It was obvious Juss had a leg injury, so he showed us how to use the hoist sitting on the smaller stools on wheels, standing up, or for Juss' height on his scooter.

Then, of course, when I was talking deals and dollars with Connor, Juss and Sparra raced each other from one end of the shop to the other. Sparra was on the wheelie-stool and Juss was on his scooter and, of course, Juss won, so there was a bit of yelling and laughing, and both Connor and I stopped to watch them.

To see Juss laughing and so full of life, after being near-catatonic a week ago, made me happier than words could say.

Then it was Davo's turn to race Juss, but his scooter was faster than a little stool. Not to mention that Juss had it down to an art.

"Seem like a fun bunch," Connor said.

"Anything with wheels, I swear," I replied.

"The guy with the mobility scooter," he began. "Leg injury?"

Amongst other things. "Yep."

"Motorbike?"

"Nah. The van he was driving got hit by a truck."

"Holy hell," he whispered. Then the penny dropped. "Oh shit, was that a few months back? I remember that. It was on the news. They weren't expecting him to survive. And that's him?"

"Yep."

"Wow, he was lucky." Then he cringed. "Not that getting hit by a truck is lucky . . ."

"We were all lucky that day," I answered. "Lucky he survived, that is."

We watched on as Juss laughed at something Davo said, and my heart flooded with warmth. *We came so close to losing him.*

I signed off on two new hoists, feeling pretty good about upgrading shop equipment for the guys. When we came out of my office, they had Juss' bike off the hoist and Justin was sitting on it.

"Looks like he misses not being able to ride," Connor said to me, and after a bit of small talk and promises to be in touch real soon, Davo and Sparra helped him load the demo hoists back into his truck, and he left.

Juss was grinning as he sat on his bike, and it was hard not to smile back at him. "I'm telling ya," he said. "One day."

I nodded. "One day." Then what Connor had said and seeing Juss smile like that gave me an idea. "Can you put your foot on the footpeg okay?"

He lifted his right leg and bent it so he could put his foot up. "Yeah. But if I had to stop in a hurry and put my leg down . . ."

"Hold on," I said. I ducked into my office and came back out holding up the key.

"Dallas, I . . ." He shook his head.

"You're not going to. I am. You just gotta hold onto me."

"You're gonna double me?"

"Just out through the shop, around the backyard, and back in. We're not going out on the street."

There was a moment of hesitation before his grin widened. "Hell. Yes."

I grabbed our helmets and put mine on, then handed Juss his. "If it's uncomfortable . . ."

He gently fitted the helmet over his scar, and when he had it on, he grinned so hard, his cheeks barely fit in the helmet. I swung my leg over the tank and handlebars, stood astride, kicked up the stand, and took control of the weight of the bike.

Juss put his hands on my hips, then around my waist. "I like this," he said.

I put the key in the ignition and turned her over. The bike spluttered a bit and kicked to life, and Davo and Sparra raced into the shop. Davo sagged when he saw it was me.

"You scared the shit outta me! Thought it was Jusso," he yelled over the sound of the engine.

I tapped the gears down into first and released the clutch, nice and easy. We rolled forward and puttered out past Davo and Sparra—who were grinning madly—through the front roller door into the yard, then around the back near my ute, and through the rear roller door. I made the loop a second time before driving back into the workshop and coming to a stop and turning the engine off.

Sparra helped Juss off the bike, and I took my helmet off, waiting to see Juss' face.

I don't know how he got his helmet off with the way he was grinning. "That was so awesome! Thank you!"

"Oh God, you've created a monster," Sparra said. "He's gonna wanna do it all the time now. And then it'll be on his own. And then it'll be on a motocross track."

Juss was on too much of a high to care. "No, no. Not yet. But that . . . being on a bike again." He met my eyes and nodded. "That's who I am."

Oh, Juss.

Davo clapped him on the shoulder. "How do you feel? Vibrations didn't rattle anything loose?"

"Nah. Feel good."

He was still grinning when he called it a day before lunch. I went upstairs with him and he was just buzzing. He went to the kitchen and leaned against the kitchen bench. "Dall, that was so good. I know it was for like, half a minute. But being on a bike, the sound of it, the smell of the exhaust. The way it feels, that exhilaration. I remember that. Even when I was a kid and things were shit at home, having a bike was what kept me sane. I'd work on it, ride it, tune it. Being on a bike is . . . me."

I kissed him with smiling lips. "I should have thought about doing it sooner."

"I dunno if I was ready before now. I might have freaked out, and for a second I was scared when you first mentioned it. Because what if I came off and got hurt again. But I trust you, and then I wanted to do it." He shook his head like he couldn't believe it. "And Dall, it was . . . It was good to be reminded of who I am. It's not like getting a memory back, not really. More of a confirmation or reassurance that I'm still me."

I wrapped my arms around him and gave him the biggest hug. "I'm so happy for you, Juss. Seeing you smile like that means the world to me."

He sighed. "I told you it was going to be a good week."

I held him for a bit longer, just because I could. "Want me to make you a sandwich?"

He pulled back and looked up at me. His eyes were bright and clear. Happy. "Nah, I got it. You better get back downstairs. You've got a parts delivery coming this arvo, and Sparra wasn't done with that engine rebuild."

"Maybe if someone wasn't racing him on his scooter," I joked.

"I beat him too. And Davo."

I kissed him with smiling lips. "I know. I watched."

"I'll be down later, before knock-off time. I need a nap, and I can't decide if Squish and I are gonna watch some TV or if I'll watch some porn."

I snorted. "Okay then. Well, I'll let you decide." I got to the door and turned back to face him. "But if you wanted to wait until tonight, maybe we could both watch it?"

His smile became something else and he readjusted himself. "Today's the best day ever."

"WELL, you certainly look a lot better than the last time I saw you," Doctor Chang said, clearly surprised to see Justin in such good shape.

"I feel so much better," Juss said. "Honestly."

Doctor Chang studied him for a second. "When I saw you last week, you weren't feeling too great."

"No, I wasn't," he replied. "And I didn't leave the hospital too great either. I was pretty much wiped out for three days, literally couldn't get off the couch, but I got better every day. I rested, drank a lot of water, ate well, slept a lot." He squeezed my hand and gave me a smile before turning back to the doc. "Not gonna lie, it scared the hell outta me. Scared Dall, too."

She gave a nod and a small smile aimed at me. "I know. I saw him. I don't know which one of you looked worse."

"Yeah, it wasn't much fun," I said.

Juss' hold on my hand tightened. "That's why I don't want to ever go through that again. I don't want to put myself through it, because it sucked, but . . . God, when I woke up in hospital and saw his face, he looked wrecked. I can't do that to him again."

"I'm glad to hear that," she said. "Did you want to talk about what you felt during the episode or what you experienced?"

He shrugged. "I felt . . . stuck. Like before, after the accident, with the mist, it kind of swirled and moved. But this was thick and heavy, almost like being underwater. I could see and hear but I couldn't get anything to make sense. I couldn't speak. I just couldn't do anything. There was no room in my head because it was so full of fog."

He'd used that analogy before, with the mist and fog. "But it cleared away pretty quick this time."

Doctor Chang nodded. "It's not uncommon that patients recover quickly from something such as this. It's more of a stumble than a full reset to square one. But we don't want to be making a habit out of it, or the recovery times may start to lag."

"I don't want to go through it again," Juss said again. "Whatever I have to do."

She smiled and went through a list of procedures. How to recognise triggers and how to reduce the harm factor. And how to cope with stress and anxiety, and how to relieve the pressure of an attack.

Juss nodded keenly at everything she said and suggested. "Okay. I can do that. And Dall will help notice any changes that I can't see."

"For sure," I agreed. "And I'll not wait next time."

"Good, because, Justin, I'm writing you a referral for a therapist. She's brilliant and—"

"A therapist?" he asked.

"Yes." Her gaze was unwavering. "We need to treat your mental health as we do your physical health. Not only in dealing with recognising stress triggers, but also with dealing with the accident. This is a long-term health treatment, and one I recommend to all my patients."

I squeezed his hand. "We can do that."

"So you mentioned your mother is one trigger," Doctor Chang said, writing something down.

"Yeah. We blocked her number so she can't call me anymore," Justin said. "It really helps just knowing I did that."

"Less anxiety hanging over you," Doctor Chang said.

"Every time the phone rings because you know it can't be her."

"Exactly."

"Good. Okay, so in the event of a stressful situation, what are some things you enjoy that could help relax you?"

"Sex," Justin replied. "Please say sex."

Doctor Chang's eyes went wide and I snorted out a laugh. "Juss."

"No, babe, I'm serious. If she tells me it's a coping mechanism, then it's technically doctor's orders, and then we can have sex all the time."

I laughed again and put my hand to my forehead. "Sorry, Doc."

She chuckled too. "Don't apologise. Justin, you had some anxiety before from just the idea of sex. I take it you've been working on that?"

"Uh, yeah," he replied. "The small-steps approach worked well. Very well, actually. So if you could, you know, say it has medicinal purposes . . ."

She smiled at that. "A doctor's recommendation?"

He didn't hesitate. "Yes, please."

"As long as it doesn't elevate stress or pain levels—"

"Oh, it doesn't," he said, cutting her off. "And I do feel very relaxed afterward."

"Oh God." I wanted the floor to open up and swallow me. "Juss, baby."

Doctor Chang fought a smile. "Sex can increase the body's production of oxytocin which releases endorphins."

Juss nodded. "Yes, it can."

"And that has been proven to reduce stress," she added. *Jesus, she was going along with this.* "But Justin, you should know that having a partner isn't required for sexual release. You don't technically require Dallas' assistance."

"Well, that's true," Juss replied. He let go of my hand and put both his hands out as though he was about to explain the size of a fish. "But he has a dick—"

I pulled his hand down, mortified. "Oh my God, you're not finishing that."

Doctor Chang burst out laughing and blushed a dark pink. "Well," she said. "I won't call it doctor's orders, but a . . . recommendation." Then she grew serious. "And only if it's consensual between both of you. If Dallas isn't comfortable, Justin, masturbation is fine."

"Oh, it's consensual," Juss replied cheerfully. "Isn't it, Dall?"

I sighed and shook my head with a laugh. "In case you were wondering, Doc, this whole conversation is a *very* Justin kind of conversation."

He smiled at me. "I feel good. I feel like me, like I can say the things I want to say. I wondered for a while who I was, and I wondered what version of me Dallas fell in love with. And now I know."

"The real you," I answered.

He nodded. "Yep." He sat back in his seat and sighed, looking right at Doctor Chang. "There is going to be so much sex tonight."

She smiled at us and closed his file. Our time was up. "I want to see you again next week. I know I said we could move to fortnightly appointments, but after last week, I'd just like to make sure we follow-up properly."

Justin looked to me. "She wants an update on the sex."

She put up her hands. "No, I don't. Unless there's an issue we need to discuss, or if you have anything you'd like to talk about. But no details," she said, putting her hands out like Justin had done with the size thing. "And no bragging, cripes."

That made Justin laugh, and it made me blush. "Sorry about that," I said. Christ, I could not believe that was a topic of conversation . . .

We left the appointment and made our way home. Justin reached over the console to take my hand while I drove. "There will be bragging. I hope she knows that."

I snorted. "Pretty sure she does, yeah."

# CHAPTER TWELVE

WE GOT BACK to the shop and Juss wanted to help
Sparra with the ATV he was working on, citing he'd rest
after lunch. He and Sparra had always been good mates,
and since his accident, Juss had easily fallen back into step
with him.

It helped that Sparra was easy going and never batted
an eyelid that Juss couldn't remember him from before. If he
had to explain something again, he'd just tell it like it was
the first time.

And I shouldn't have been surprised when Juss had said
he and Sparra were going to walk down to the corner takeaway shop and grab us some burgers. Sure, they delivered,
but Juss and Sparra wanted to walk and chat, and after all,
they'd done it a hundred times. But not since the accident.

"We'll be fine," Juss said to me. "I'm using the scooter."

And what could I say? He was an adult, for crying out
loud. I couldn't tell him no. I wasn't his keeper.

"Okay then, well, be safe. And if you need me, call me."

Juss rolled his eyes but he smiled. "Dall, I'll be fine."

I nodded, because yeah, sure, I knew he would be. And

he was cautious about overdoing it, and I knew he wouldn't push himself. But damn, I could still worry.

I watched the front gate as they left and I watched it every minute they were gone.

Davo clapped me on the back. "He'll be fine."

"Hmm."

"You gotta let him do stuff."

"I know. I just . . ."

"You just worry. I get it. And I don't blame ya. But it's just down the road, he has his scooter, and Sparra won't let anything happen to him."

"Hmm."

"He needs to be able to go into a shop and order and pay for stuff, Dall. He's gotta start doing that shit some time."

"Yeah, I know . . ." And I *did* know that. "But God, if something were to happen . . . if he falls or gets dizzy, or hears a car screech its tyres and freaks out, or—" I shook my head. "I can't bear the thought of him having another setback."

Davo's tone softened. "I know, mate. And I'm not down-playing anything that he went through or what you went through with him. But you can't be there every minute of forever. He needs to start doing things on his own again."

I sighed. "I know."

"How're you gonna be when he starts to drive again?"

I shot Davo a look that probably bordered on panicked and wild. "Christ. I dunno. I'm going to not think about that until I have to, is what I'm gonna do."

He chuckled. "You've got a bit of time yet. But you're gonna have to think about it eventually."

"Hmm." Fucking hell. "I don't want to wrap him up in cotton wool, and I know he's not made of glass. But he's not *un*breakable either. When you come so close to losing some-one, something inside you changes. You'll do anything to protect them. And when you watch them struggle every day, you want to make sure they never have to struggle again. The smallest thing to you and me could see him on bedrest for a week." *Or in hospital, almost catatonic.* I shrugged. "I'm always gonna worry. It's just part of who I am."

Davo nodded to the front gate. "Well, you can stop worrying for now."

And sure enough, Juss and Sparra were back. They were laughing at something, and he looked so happy, a pang of guilt lanced me. He should be doing things with his mates, and I felt bad for maybe shielding him a little too hard.

My face must have said as much, because Davo gave me a nudge. "It's all good, Dallas. He needs someone looking out for him."

"Haven't you two done any work while we've been gone," Sparra joked as they came in through the roller door. "I leave for thirty minutes and the work ethic goes to shit."

Davo threw his oil rag at him and we laughed as we headed into the breakroom. And all the worry aside, Juss' smile told me all I needed to know.

He needed to enjoy the good times while they were good, because Lord knew he'd had enough bad times.

We ate our lunch and Sparra gave us a rundown of how things were going with Carissa, and I'd just finished my burger when the phone rang.

I left them to keep talking for the rest of their lunch break and took the call in my office. "Muller Mechanical. Dallas speaking."

"I need to speak to Justin Keith, please."

The voice was horrible and familiar and it took a second for me to place it. It was Justin's mother. I stopped cold; anger ran like ice through my veins. I wanted to do evil to this woman, but I remembered all too well that my temper and yelling at her were partly to blame for Justin's meltdown. So I kept my voice calm and neutral. "Janet."

"Hmm, Dallas," she said, and I could just picture her sneering as she spoke my name. "I assume you're the reason he won't answer his mobile when I call it."

"I don't care what you assume."

She was quiet a second and decided to try again. "Don't suppose Justin's calmed down enough to speak to his mother?"

"Calmed down?" I asked incredulously. *Don't yell, Dallas. Don't yell.* With a deep breath, I tried to be composed. "Do you have any idea what stress and high blood pressure can do to someone with a brain injury?"

She was quiet for a second. "What?"

"Justin went to hospital in an ambulance after your little stunt last week. He couldn't speak or do anything. Ever seen someone you love catatonic like that, Janet?"

"I don't know what you're talking about," she snapped.

"I'm talking about brain injury. You know, what Justin has, if you even care. Something he has to live with forever, something that is affected by high levels of stress. Like you turning up demanding money."

"I deserve that money."

"You know what you fucking deserve?" I began, my jaw clenched.

But then I noticed Juss standing at the door. His smile was rueful. "Is that my mother?"

Goddammit.

I nodded, and he held out his hand for the phone. "Are you sure?" I asked.

"Yeah. I'll be okay, Dall."

I handed the phone over and he put it to his ear. "Mum," he said. "I'm sorry."

I shot him a look. What the *hell* was he apologising for?

"Oh no, don't misunderstand," he said. "I said I'm sorry. Sorry I missed your head when I threw my cane at you. I thought I had better aim."

Shocked, I snorted out a laugh, but Juss wasn't done.

"If you call me again or if you turn up here again, I will call the cops. I will take a restraining order out against you. You're not my family. You disowned me." Then he smiled at me. "I have a real family, Mum, and he chose me. He chose me twice."

My heart just about burst to hear him say that. I could hear her tinny voice squawking through the receiver but he was done. He'd said what he needed to say. While she was ranting away, he simply disconnected the call and slid the phone onto the desk with satisfying finality. *He was done.* I stood up and stepped around my desk to throw my arms around him in a crushing hug. I whispered into his neck, "Baby, I would choose you a hundred times."

"And I'd choose you," he replied.

I pulled back and put my hand to the side of his face and thumbed the scar above his eyebrow. "I'm sorry you had to go through that. I know your mother's been horrible, but it still sucks that you had to do that. Do you feel okay?"

"Dall, I'm fine." He smiled sadly. "I actually feel good about telling her that, like a weight has been lifted. I think when she just showed up and started yelling, I was shocked and I wasn't prepared at all. But I am now. I know what she's after, and I know you'll protect me."

"I will."

"And like you said, we find our own family."

I kissed him. "I like the sound of that. You and me."

"And Squish."

I snorted. "And Squish."

"Who is probably wondering where I am and why I've missed our nap time."

"Then you better go let him know you're okay."

"I am tired," he murmured. "And I need all the rest I can get for tonight."

"For tonight?" Then I remembered as soon as I'd said it.

"Oh yeah, and don't think you're getting out of it. It's doctor's orders."

"Pretty sure it was just a recommendation."

He gave me a lopsided smile, full of cheek and daring. "Well, it's my recommendation that you don't hold out on me." Then he was serious. He whispered, "It's my first time, Dall. My first proper time without a condom. Not just with you, but ever. I've never done that before. I mean, I have, we have, obviously. But I don't remember it. Well, I can remember that time at Hallidays Point, but I want to feel it now. I want to experience it, firsthand, and make new memories."

I lifted his chin and kissed him softly. "I have no intention of holding out on you." Then I winked at him. "I just hope your expectations and my *actual* capabilities are on par."

He chuckled. "I hear practice makes perfect."

"I might need it," I said with a laugh. Then I sighed. "You sure you feel okay about your mum?" I needed to be sure . . .

"Yeah. Actually, I feel good about it. I needed to say that

to her. Whether she listens is up to her, but I said what I needed to say."

I studied his eyes for a moment. They were a clear brown, tired, but there was no blankness, no sadness. "Okay, baby. I'll just be here. If you need anything or want to talk, I'll come straight up."

He glanced around to make sure no one could overhear. "What if I need help watching porn?"

I laughed and gave him a light smack on the arse. He smiled as he made his way upstairs, and I got back to work, grateful for the distraction. I didn't need to be thinking about what we might be doing tonight. The last thing I needed was to be working with a semi.

But between bikes, ATVs, and the never-ending phone calls, I was more than distracted. It was good, though. It felt . . . good.

Like maybe—and I didn't want to jinx myself—that life was beginning to look up. Maybe we could plateau for a bit and find our new normal. Now that we'd identified some of Justin's triggers, we could avoid them and manage them. Hopefully, his mother would now leave us alone, and he could just concentrate on getting better.

I knew it had only been a week since his last episode, and I knew it could all be different in another week. But I wanted to believe the worst was behind us.

I wanted to make sure it was.

JUSS CAME BACK DOWNSTAIRS JUST before closing. I was finishing up some paperwork and heard his laughter in the workshop. God, it made me smile. He helped the guys clean up and lock everything down for me, and Davo said he'd lock the gate as they left. Juss pulled the roller door down and came to lean against the doorframe to the office.

"They said they'd see you in the morning," he said.

"Oh, okay. I'm just getting things ready for Toni. It's her first day tomorrow."

"Yeah, the boys were talking about it. Davo reckons you're too much of a control freak and you'll still be trying to do everything and driving Toni mad."

I laughed incredulously. "A control freak?" Then I thought about that and how I'd run everything my way for years. "Yeah, okay. So maybe he's not entirely wrong. But I gotta say, Juss, I'm looking forward to handing things over."

"You are?"

"Yep. The creditors, debtors, inventory, phone calls . . . my God, the phone didn't stop ringing today. Now I'm used to the idea of someone doing all that for me, for us, I think I'm really gonna like it." I sat back in my desk chair and sighed. "I just want some time to breathe, ya know? So it's not a madhouse every day, trying to get everything done. I'll still have all my responsibilities, of course, but I want to be able to enjoy working on some bikes, having a laugh with the boys, and spending time with you. We've talked about cutting back on stress for you, and it's about time I cut some stress from my life too."

He smiled. "That sounds really good to me."

"We ready to go upstairs?"

"Babe, I'm so ready for you to take me upstairs."

I barked out a laugh. "Right, then."

"No, I mean it. I'm *ready* ready. I took care of the pipes, if you know what I mean."

It took me a second. "Oh my God, right."

He chuckled and raised an eyebrow. "Are you having second thoughts?"

"Hell no."

"Then what are you waiting for?"

I shut down my computer and stood up. "Absolutely nothing." I walked to him and kissed him soundly. "Get your arse upstairs."

He grinned. "That's more like it."

I followed him up, getting a perfect close-up view of his arse, and it didn't take my dick long to notice either. The anticipation was going to kill me. He'd wanted this for weeks and I was beginning to think I might not live up to his expectations.

When we were inside, he took one look at me and laughed. "Dall, you're overthinking this."

"You have expectations now. You're probably thinking this is gonna move both heaven and earth, and I'm seriously thinking it's gonna be over in like, five minutes. Maybe four."

He laughed again and took my hand, pulling me close. "Babe. You know me, right?"

I nodded. "Yeah."

"You know what I like, and you know how I like it. You've had years of experience with me, and I have none with you. It's the only time I'll let you use my amnesia against me." He chuckled and pulled me down for a kiss. "I have no expectations, honestly." Then he made a face. "Well, that's not true. I have two expectations. One, that you'll take it easy on me. My body isn't as flexible as it used to be. And two, that you will come inside me. I need to know what that feels like."

I gasped, his words sending a jolt of desire to my balls that almost buckled my knees. I crushed my mouth to his, using his surprise to claim his mouth with my tongue. But he was right . . . I knew him. I knew his body, what he liked, and how he liked it.

His smile broke the kiss. Grinning now—because he knew he was getting what he wanted—he pulled on my hand and led me to the bedroom. He stopped inside the door, where I could see the bed.

Which he'd already prepared. There was a pile of pillows across the middle of the bed, covered with towels. The perfect height for me to bend him over. The lube was lying on the bed covers.

Justin smiled proudly. "I told you I was ready."

I laughed and kissed him again. "First, we need to get you naked."

The days of ripping our clothes off and fucking, rough and demanding, were done. I couldn't even pull his shirt over his head without considering his arm, and getting him out of pants had to be slow and careful because of his leg.

But I didn't mind one bit. It gave me time to kiss every reveal of skin, to savour every moment. And getting him onto the bed was an exercise in caution. Once upon a time, I'd have just thrown him on the bed and crawled on after him, but not anymore.

He needed to trust that I would take care of him and make this good for him. But I also knew he couldn't endure too much for too long, so timing and endurance were important. There was a happy medium in there somewhere, and I was determined to find it.

Once I had him into position, bent over the pillows with his arse high up in the air, I rubbed his back and skimmed my hands over his arse. I poured lube onto my fingers and ran them across his hole.

He moaned.

I pushed a fingertip inside him and slowly worked him, getting his arse ready for me. Yes, I'd been inside him since the accident, but I hadn't fucked him. I hadn't thrust and stretched him like I was about to.

God, just thinking about it . . . My cock ached to be in him right now.

I worked in another finger, and then I added my tongue. He gasped and gripped the bed covers. "Oh fuck," he groaned. "Dallas, what . . . oh God."

I chuckled. "I know what you like, remember?"

He groaned, a deep guttural sound as I tongue-fucked him some more. When he began rocking his hips back and forth, I knew he was ready.

I lubed my cock and poured more over his hole, working it in with my thumb before lining my cockhead up and swiping it over his slick entrance, pushing just a little. "You ready, baby?"

"Yes. Dallas, please . . ."

So I pushed inside him, slow, so torturously slow, and he fisted the blankets and whined as I pressed in. He gasped as he took me into his body. I stilled, holding myself right there while he got used to the intrusion. I leaned over him, lay down on top of him with my cock fully seated inside him, and whispered in his ear, "Breathe, baby."

It took a moment but his breaths deepened and he relaxed, then began to roll his hips. I followed his tempo, slow and intense. He began to groan, gruff and gravelly.

That sound, so familiar and so new, told me he loved it, told me he was ready for more. So I listened to him, to his body, and set my pace in tune with his grunts, his groans, his mindless pleas for more.

I thrust in deep and pulled back slow, gently gripping

his hips and giving him every inch. Giving him exactly what he wanted. Slow, tender, and so fucking good.

He was tight and hot, slick and welcoming as I took him. Pleasure building so thick and strong, I could taste it. My cock felt like steel, so hard, my balls needed release.

"Baby, I can't hold on," I ground out, my hips thrusting of their own accord, seeking more, more, more.

"God, Dallas, do it," he panted. "Come inside me."

I thrust in one last time, every inch, and my orgasm barrelled through me. Pleasure and love overwhelmed and consumed me as I came, spilling deep inside him.

He gasped and cried out as I groaned through my release, thrusting with every pulse. I collapsed on top of him, still inside him, while the world around me spun. He gave me time to catch my breath before he began to rock his hips.

This was what he loved.

He loved my spent cock inside him, my come inside him. He loved to stay joined, coupled and close. He slid his hand underneath himself and began to fuck his fist. "Dallas, I need . . ."

"I'll give you everything you need, baby," I murmured, reaching under him. I replaced his hand around his shaft and gave him a few hard strokes.

"Oh, God."

I kept my semi-hard dick buried in him while I jacked him off, and knowing which words would send him over the edge, I whispered into the back of his neck, "Can you feel my come inside you?"

Juss stilled; his cock surged and swelled in my hand before spilling onto the towel beneath him. He cried out, trembling and convulsing with the power of his orgasm until he collapsed on the mattress.

I pressed my weight on his back, still in him. I never wanted to leave. But he'd probably overdone it and was going to be sore tomorrow. So I slowly pulled out and he whined. "Stay."

I chuckled and kissed his shoulder and behind his ear, but I kept my length pressed against him. "Baby, I don't want to hurt you."

"I can feel how hard you are."

"Because you just jerked off with my cock in your arse. It's hot as hell."

He ripped the pillows out from underneath him so he was flat on the bed. He spread his legs wider and raised his arse. "I'm not kidding, Dallas. I want more."

Fuck.

There it was. That demanding, sexual side of Justin that had been absent for so long. So I gave him what he wanted. I knelt between his thighs and gave myself a few long strokes before I pushed back into him in one, sharp thrust. He was so slick, so inviting.

He was home to me.

He moaned as I thrust in and out of him. I kissed the back of his neck, his shoulder, as I drove into him, balls deep and rocking, and I was at the edge already.

Being inside him, making love, was everything familiar and brand new all over again.

His eyes went wide when I came, and he gasped as he felt it. "Oh, God, yes. Dallas, yes."

I collapsed on top of him again, and this time I did pull out. Before he could protest, I rolled us onto our sides and wrapped him up in my arms. I kissed him, deep and with all the love and passion I had in me. And for a long time, we just lay there, kissing, holding each other, basking in what we'd just done.

He was tired though, and when he nuzzled into my neck, I stroked his back, his hip. "You're going to need that massage," I murmured. "And a hot shower. And dinner."

"Mm." He was almost asleep. "Just wanna stay right here."

I held him a bit tighter. "I love you so much," I whispered.

"Love you too, Dall." After a few moments, I felt him smile into my neck. "Love what you did to me, love how you did it."

I chuckled and traced lazy circles on his back. "You're going to be sore tomorrow."

"Worth it." He sighed and snuggled in some more. "So fucking worth it."

# CHAPTER THIRTEEN

"ARE YOU SURE YOU FEEL OKAY?" I asked. The guys were about to arrive for work and I was making sure the office was somewhat tidy for Toni before she arrived for her first day. But I needed to make sure Juss was feeling okay after last night. Again.

"Like I told you each of the ten times you've asked me already, I feel great. I'm a little achy in all the right places, but it's a good ache." He leaned over and pulled my chin up for a kiss. "And I appreciate you asking because I know you worry, and you worry because you love me. But so help me God, Dallas, if you ask me again when everyone's here, I will tell them why you're asking."

I chuckled, because that was such a Justin thing to say.

"And I will use the fire extinguisher as a size guide."

I burst out laughing just as we heard Davo drive into the yard. "Okay, I won't ask again. I trust that you'll tell me if there's something wrong."

He was pleased by that. "I will."

He pulled his scooter over and sat down, then made a

face. I raised an eyebrow. "I'm not going to ask if that hurt, but if I were to suggest some padding on that seat . . ."

He wiggled on the seat. "No, but I might be in need of another massage by tonight."

"Now, that, I can do."

"With your fire extinguisher."

Davo and Sparra walked in. "What's that about a fire extinguisher?" Davo asked. "Are we due for a safety check?"

Juss chuckled as he scooted out to greet them. "Something like that."

Toni arrived next, and after formal introductions to the team, I spent most of the morning in the office with her, showing her the ropes. I wasn't surprised that she had it all down in no time given she was answering the phone and taking bookings in her first twenty minutes on the job. She laughed with the boys at smoko time and could talk shit about bikes with the best of them.

She was a perfect fit.

After lunch, Juss called it a day and went upstairs and I followed him up. "I'm not going to ask," I began.

"I'm fine, Dall. Just tired. It's nap time for me and Squish. I'll come back down later."

"Okay then."

"Toni seems to be working out all right?" he said, getting himself on the couch.

"Yeah, she's great. She's already reorganising stuff and making spreadsheets to streamline our ordering process."

Squish came out of the bedroom and joined Juss on the couch, and Juss started flicking through channels. "Sorry, Squish," he said. "No fishing shows today. The Spanish motocross championships are on. We can watch *Fishing Australia* later."

I laughed and leaned down to kiss Juss' forehead. "Call me if you need me."

His eyelids were getting heavy already, but he gave me an easy smile. "Mm, doing booty calls now? 'Cause I think I'm gonna need more of what you did to me last night."

I laughed as I went back down to the shop, and I spent most of the afternoon working on a Honda bike that had picked up dirty fuel.

It was weird that every time the phone rang, I reached for my back pocket to take the call. Davo laughed at me a few times when he saw me, and he nodded to the office. "Wondering why you didn't hire someone years ago?"

"God, yes."

Toni still had to come and ask me questions now and then, but she mostly had it all under control. Which meant I got my work done so much quicker, and without the interruptions, I could do a better job.

Juss came back down at 3:30 and he and Sparra finished up the job they'd been working on, and I stuck my head in the office to make sure Toni was going okay. "How's your first day been?"

"Good!" she said. "Just getting things organised. I'll attack the filing cabinets and stationery cupboard tomorrow."

"Make a list of anything you need, and we'll get it."

"Oh, there's an email that came through a little while ago," she said. "About a replacement van. If you read it and tell me what you want me to say, I can draft up a reply for you."

"Oh man." My gaze automatically went to Justin, where he was talking with Sparra. "I guess that's a conversation I need to have with Juss first." I gave her a smile. "I'll let you know tomorrow, thanks."

That was a conversation I'd put off long enough.

When everyone left for the day, I locked the gate behind Toni and headed back into the workshop. Juss pulled the roller doors down and went to head into the office. "Babe, it's home time," I called out.

He stopped. "Don't you have paperwork to do for a bit?"

"Nope. Toni's got it all under control."

His eyes lit up. "So we have an early mark?"

I smiled at that. "Yep."

"I do believe there was talk of a massage."

I led him to the back stairs. "I do believe so too."

I followed him up, noting how his steps had improved. He used his leg with much more ease now, taking each tread with more confidence. I doubted he'd ever again be sprinting up them two at a time like he used to, but seeing his improvement made me smile.

We got through the door and he headed straight for the kitchen. "I was thinking we could have veggie stir fry for dinner," he began.

"Sure. Sounds great. But, uh, Juss, can we talk for a second?"

He stopped to stare at me and his face fell. "Did I do something wrong?"

*Oh, baby.* "No. Why would you think that?"

"I don't know. You just have a line between your eyebrows that you get when you're worried or thinking about serious stuff. Or when you don't want to tell me something. Like you don't want to tell me something right now . . ."

"And you thought you didn't know how to read me," I said with a smile. I took his hand and we sat at the table.

"There's nothing wrong. I just wanted to talk about the van and whether or not we should get it replaced."

He sagged a little and put his hand to his heart. "God, is that all? Shit, Dallas, you freaked me out."

"I'm sorry. I should have told you it wasn't anything about us." We'd learned the hard way that freaking Justin out didn't end well. "I'm so sorry."

"It's okay. I just panicked for a second." He took a deep breath and let out a sigh of relief. "What about the van?"

"Oh, it's just the insurance company has requested some information about whether or not we want the van replaced. And I wanted to ask you."

"Me?"

"Well, yeah. I guess I need to know if you want—not now, but when you're ready—to replace the mobile mechanic van, and if you wanted to do it again."

"Me, drive?"

"When you're given the all-clear."

He frowned. "I don't know. I haven't thought about it."

"Yeah, and you don't need to answer right now. You certainly don't have to do it if you don't want."

Juss thought for a long few seconds, then shook his head sadly. "I don't think I could. Be a mobile mechanic again. I mean, not on my own, for a long time. I can't lift a lot of things, and physically, I just don't think I could."

"It's okay, baby. You don't have to decide right now. You don't need to worry about it or stress over it. You can say no now, and in a year's time or five years' time, if you want to think about it again, that's okay too."

His gaze locked to mine and he nodded. "Thanks. I just . . . I'm not ready. I can't drive yet anyway, and . . ."

"And?"

"And I don't know how I feel about driving." He put his

hand to his forehead. "I mean, I'll probably drive again at some point, but I can't . . . I get so tired and I can't concentrate too much for too long. My reflexes are kinda slow, and the idea of being in another accident scares the shit outta me, if I'm being honest. Or causing one. God, what if I hurt someone?"

I cupped his face and kissed him before pulling him in for a long, hard hug. "It's okay, baby. You don't need to worry about it right now. I just need to tell the insurance people what we planned on doing and wanted to ask you first. The mobile van was your idea, and it was your thing."

He was quiet while I held him and I rubbed his back, giving him time to think and relax.

"What do you want me to do?" he asked eventually. "As my boyfriend? And as my boss? Are they different things here?"

I pulled back and put my forehead to his so he had to look at me. "Boyfriend first, always. We've never had an issue with lines or boundaries, and I don't want to start now. I would never make you do something you weren't comfortable doing, as a boyfriend or a boss, okay?"

"I know. I'm sorry. I just wasn't sure . . . I didn't know how I should answer."

"The truth, Juss. Whatever you feel."

He gave a small smile. "You don't want me to do it, do you?"

I sighed. "And you said you couldn't read me."

He smiled at that. "Guess I'm learning."

"Baby, I don't know how I feel about you driving at all." I admitted. "I'd be happy to scrap the van altogether. I don't want to risk any more accidents, and as a boss, I have to think about those things. It's just not worth anyone else going through this. But as a boyfriend, the idea of you even driving on your own scares me right now. I know I can't wrap you up in cotton wool, and even small things like you walking to the take-out shop with Sparra was enough to freak me out. That's something I have to work on, I know that. You have to have your independence, and you can do whatever you want. But the thought of you being hurt again just terrifies me. The thought of you being hurt and me not being there to help you terrifies me even more." I sighed, long and loud. "I know I can't be there all the time, and I know I can't fix every single thing. But . . ."

"But you're a control freak and you can't help that."

I snorted. "Exactly."

His gaze flickered between mine. "Remember when Doctor Chang said fear of more pain stopped me from wanting to have sex? Well, it's a bit like that for you. Not the sex part, obviously. But after the accident, you went through hell too. And you're just trying to do whatever you can to never experience that again. I get that. Believe me."

I got a little teary, and I nodded. "Yeah. But like you said; you'll probably drive again someday and we'll have to work on that. I don't want my fear to stop you from doing anything."

"Small steps is what she suggested."

"Small steps." I nodded. "I can do small steps."

He smiled and relaxed with a deep sigh. "So we can agree on maybe one day but not right now."

I kissed him. "Agreed." He slotted in against me once more and wrapped his arms around me, giving me one helluva hug. "Hey, I thought I was the resident best-hug giver. Are you trying to take my title?"

He chuckled. "You smell like petrol, grease, and dirt. And sweat."

"Sorry. I should shower."

He held me tighter. "Absolutely not. I love that smell. A mechanic smell, my favourite kind. You could bottle it." Then he ran his hand down to my arse and gave me a squeeze. "Or we could be naked and you can rub that scent all over me." My dick twitched and, of course, he felt it. He laughed. "Someone liked that idea."

I nuzzled into his neck and whispered against his ear. "How sore do you want to be tomorrow?"

He chuckled and moaned as he craned his neck, giving me more skin to kiss and nip. "You'll just have to massage me all better."

I scraped my teeth along his jaw before capturing his mouth with mine. He moaned into my mouth and melted against me, so pliable, so giving.

I led him to our bedroom, stripped us both naked, and laid him face down on the mattress. He wanted a massage, so that's what I gave him. I worshipped every inch of him until he was begging me to fill him. So then I gave him that too.

THE NEXT FEW days were blissful. Work was great: having Toni in the office was a godsend and everyone was less stressed all round. The new hoists were delivered on Friday and I ordered pizza for everyone at lunch, and Juss and the boys had more races on the new stools. I don't think we stopped smiling all day.

And the next few weeks were much the same. Justin's appointments with Doctor Chang were now only once a fortnight, and Megan only had to do one homecare visit a week. He met his new therapist and was pleased they'd worked on a long-term plan together. He kept doing his physio exercises and he was walking more and more. His strength was increasing every day, and although he still only worked until lunchtime, he was doing a lot more. He'd still take his nap with Squish every day, then come back down and help us finish up. That schedule probably wouldn't change for a long time, and that was perfectly okay with me.

He didn't get any new memories or flashbacks, and given he hadn't had any in over a month, it was becoming less likely he ever would.

And that was okay too.

Somewhere along the way he'd made peace with that. He had all the memories he needed, he'd said. He was more focused on living in the present, making new memories here and now, and planning for the future.

I certainly couldn't argue with that.

Jimmy and Nancy had invited us again to their next family lunch, and Justin had enjoyed it just as much as last time. The same familiar faces were there, plus a few new ones, and Juss wasn't so tired this time. At first, I might have thought it a little odd that he and Jimmy had formed some kind of bond. He was the driver of the truck that hit Justin's van, after all. But Juss bonded with Nancy too, and all their kids who were all our age, or a bit older. Then it occurred to me what it was . . .

Justin had found himself a part of a family. And me too, I guessed. But maybe they were like the parents he'd never had, the fondness and affection he needed from his own mother and never got.

When Juss had told Nancy what had happened with his mum, she'd hugged him fiercely and basically swept him under her wing with all the other kids like a clutch of chicks. And Juss had just positively beamed.

"I really like them," he said as we got home. "They're just such good people."

"They are," I said, getting out of the ute. "I bet Jimmy was a real looker in his younger days."

Juss had smiled at that, but then he was quiet a while, which I put down to his being tired. He parked himself on the couch but didn't fall asleep straight away. He stared at the TV, though he wasn't really watching it, while I folded the clothes from the dryer. His brow furrowed, which told me he was overthinking something.

"Everything okay?" I asked, sitting down beside him.

"Yeah." He took my hand and studied his fingers as they threaded with mine. "Just thinking about something Jimmy said today."

"What was that?"

"When he toasted to family and all that."

I thought the whole family thing had been on his mind and it would seem I wasn't wrong. "I think they include you in their family now."

He smiled, tired but happy. "I think so too. I like that."

"I do too. I know it means a lot to you."

"It does. I mean, I have Becca and the girls. And I have you."

"You do."

"And you said something once about found family."

"Yep. The people who choose you. They love you because they want to, not because they have to."

His hold on my hand tightened and a worry line formed between his brows.

"Juss, what is it? What's the matter?" He tried to swallow and struggled, and for a heart-stopping second, I thought he was having another turn. "Juss?"

"I'm okay, I just . . ." He let out a shaky breath. "I don't know how to ask this. It kinda feels wrong to ask, like I'm asking too much. But then it feels so right . . ."

"Baby, you can ask me anything. Anything at all."

His soulful brown eyes met mine. "Would you marry me?"

I stared at him, shocked, stunned, speechless. I was not expecting that, and it took me a second to form words. "Marry you?"

"Yeah, sorry. I know it's a lot to ask, given—" He waved his hand at his head, namely his scar. "And I probably should have asked a better way, like more romantic, but I'm pretty sure if I tried to set something romantic up, I would've freaked out trying to organise it and keep it secret from you. Probably would have had another meltdown, actually. And today, all that talk about family . . . I mean, you're my family. You're my everything. And I want it to be official and real, and we can get married now; you said we could—"

I kissed him quiet. "Yes."

It took him a second. "Yes?"

"Yes." I nodded and my eyes burned with tears. "My God, yes. I would love to marry you. Nothing would make me happier." I kissed him again. My heart was thumping against my ribs, I was so giddy! But he'd said something first . . . "But before I get too excited, why would you say it's a lot to ask?"

"Because of my injuries," he replied like it was obvious. "Because chances are, I'm gonna have some cognitive issues later in life. Around Jimmy's age, probably. And asking you to sign up for that probably isn't really fair."

"Justin, I love you. Nothing's gonna change that. In sickness and in health, or however it goes. That's what love means. Please don't ever doubt me."

"I don't doubt you, Dall. You're the one true thing in my life. Out of all the fog and fear and loss, was you. I can't imagine my life or my future without you. I want to marry you and wear your ring and be yours in every way I can. Maybe not just yet. I mean, I'd marry you right now if you wanted, but just knowing is enough for now. I don't want to overload my brain, but just knowing we're a kind of family is all I need."

"We were already a kind of family, Juss."

"But this makes it real." He shrugged and made a face. "In my head. I don't know why. But legally too. The government can't say we're not a family if we get married. And hospitals and insurances can't say we're not a family either."

"Oh, baby."

"If something were to happen, Dall," he whispered. "I need you with me. But it's not all just doom and gloom. I want to be yours for all the fun stuff too, I want to be married to you, to be your husband."

I kissed him again. "And I'll be yours."

Juss' eyes filled with tears and he began to cry. "You'll really marry me?"

"Yes, baby. A thousand times yes." I thumbed away his tears. "Why are you crying?"

"All I ever wanted was a family of my own."

"Oh, Jussy." I pulled him into a hug. "We are a family. Married or not, you and me, we're a family."

He sobbed and sniffled. "And Squish."

"Yeah, baby. And Squish too."

He inhaled deeply and settled into me, like he could finally relax. I held him until he fell asleep, and even then I still didn't get up. I let him sleep with his face smooshed into my chest, his hands tucked in between us, and I wrapped him up in my arms and let the realisation of what just happened settle over us like a warm blanket.

We were gonna get married. He wanted to marry me, to make it official, to make it real. He still seemed to think he wasn't worthy, so obviously I would need to spend the next fifty or sixty years proving to him that he was.

He asked me to marry him. And no, I didn't need any fancy proposal or grand romantic gesture. That wasn't who we were. We were just two knock-around blokes trying to make sense of life, together. All we needed was each other.

Squish chose that very moment to join us, jumping up onto the couch, already purring and looking for the best place to curl up with Juss. "Yes, you too."

"ARE YOU READY?"

"I am so ready."

Dallas grinned. "Me too. You nervous?"

I inhaled deeply and let it out real slow. We were dressed in matching navy dress pants and white button-up shirts and shined dress shoes. It didn't hurt that Dallas' shirt was tight and showed his muscly chest and biceps. And how his pants hugged him in all the right places. His hair was freshly cut, his beard trimmed, and he was handsome as hell. "Nope. I'm excited. Why? Are you nervous?"

"A little bit. Just about speaking in front of people, that's all."

"Don't be. We've got this."

He shook his head, smiling. "Since when did you become the expert?"

"I had a good teacher."

That was true. The last two years had been amazing and sometimes hard, but mostly great. If we could call it a climb, then the view from the top was spectacular. It hadn't all been easy. I'd had ongoing physio but my leg was as good as new now, and there'd been ongoing neuro follow-ups, scans, appointments, and therapy sessions. I still had to watch stress levels, and doing too much and overworking my brain would put me back on my arse for a while. And, of course, the headaches were still a thing.

I never did get all my memory back. I got some random bits and pieces, some flashbacks that hit me out of nowhere, but there were still holes in my timeline, but there was nothing I could do about it. I had to accept that. I could either spend time and energy being mad about it, or I could put that time and energy into making new memories. It wasn't really a choice.

I hadn't had another episode. I hadn't had any worrying downfalls or major setbacks. And that was, without any doubt, for me at least, because of Dallas.

He'd disagree with that and say it was because we knew how to address stress now, but we all knew it was the truth.

My prognosis was good, though I would always be a traumatic brain injury survivor. The likelihood of me having issues later in life was always a possibility, but we were aware and proactive with my health. The truth was, Dallas was right, like he usually was. We were in this together, always, no matter what life threw at us.

I'd come up with a plan for my money, and that was to let it sit earning interest until Dallas and I were ready to sell the business and move on. That wasn't going to be for a long while away, another twenty or thirty years, God willing. We debated over buying a house somewhere close to the shop, but we loved the flat upstairs. We loved being close to work, and it meant I could easily go home if I needed to rest, without driving. But maybe one day we would move, when we were looking to retire, and the money was my safety net.

And if that had to include funds, should I need medical care later in life, then so be it.

It was just what we'd have to do. Like everything, we'd do it together.

*Together, forever.*

"I think they're waiting for us to start," Dallas said.

I held out my hand for him to take and looked down at myself. "Do I look okay?"

"You're sexy as fuck," he said, stepping in for a kiss.

"Okay, you two, Jesus H Christ," Sparra said, interrupting us. "We're all over here waiting and you two are here making out."

He said it loud enough so people could hear, and, of course, they laughed. I chuckled and took a deep breath and held out my hand. "Okay, Mr Muller. Let's do this."

Dallas grasped my hand, holding on tight. "It is my honour to walk down this aisle with you."

He made my heart skip a beat, or ten. God, we were finally getting married. And yes, we chose to walk each other down the aisle. We didn't exactly have willing parents, but we also wanted to begin our married lives as equal partners.

We'd asked just our closest friends and family to attend our wedding. Becca and the girls were there, of course, but my mother most certainly never received an invitation. I don't even know if she knew about the wedding.

I'd seen her once since I'd cut her off. I ran into her downtown and she was as surprised to see me as I was her. She looked around for Dallas and smiled when she realised he wasn't with me. "Boyfriend not leeching off you today?" she'd sneered.

"You mean fiancé?" I'd replied with a bright smile.

"He's always with me. He, unlike you, would never abandon me."

Her expression turned sour, but I was done with it. I was done with her. I was about to remind her that I'd call the cops if I had to, to keep her away from me, but instead I turned and walked away.

I hadn't seen or heard of her since.

Becca hadn't spoken to her much over the last two years either, so it was more than likely that my mother didn't even know I was getting married.

And for that, I was glad.

I had my found family, and today I was making it official.

Davo and Lauren sat at the front with little Elliott on Lauren's knee. Elliott was dressed in a little vest and pants outfit that matched Davo's as if it wasn't the cutest thing ever. Davo becoming a dad was the best thing to ever happen to him, and he was full of advice for Sparra, because he and Carissa were expecting their first baby any day now.

That made me and Dallas uncles, and I'd be lying if I said I didn't love it.

Kids weren't something Dall and I wanted, but that didn't mean we couldn't love and spoil them rotten.

Jimmy and Nancy were in the second row, dressed up all fancy and beaming like proud parents. Dallas' dad and step-mum were there, and Mark, one of his brothers. They didn't have an overly great relationship, but the fact they'd come today meant a lot to Dallas.

Our wedding was on Dixon Park Beach, overlooking the Pacific, where Dallas had brought me a few times since the accident to relax and soak up some sun. When he'd suggested it as a location, I couldn't think of anywhere better.

There was a small congregation of white chairs and a celebrant who stood at the end in between two tall stands of white flowers. Everything looked so simple and perfect, and admittedly, I'd had a lot of help from Toni with everything. I think she took pity on us and did most of the organising.

But the whole thing was perfect. It was a beautiful spring day, the ocean was sparkling, the sun was shining, and some passers-by had gathered a safe distance to watch. We met the celebrant at the front and the ceremony began.

"I'd like to thank everyone for coming today to witness the union of Dallas and Justin," the celebrant said. "And don't worry, everyone. I've been told they wanted the ceremony short and sweet because, and I quote Dallas on this, 'No one likes that drawn-out, boring stuff.'"

That earned us a chuckle, but honestly, it was true. So the celebrant gave a quick spiel about the sanctity of marriage and love and acceptance, and before we knew it, it was time for our vows.

Dallas and I turned to face each other, our hands joined between us, and I'd never seen him so nervous! I rubbed the backs of his hands with my thumbs and he gave me a thankful smile. "I'm supposed to be going first," he said. "That was a bad idea, oh my God."

I chuckled. "You're okay," I whispered. "Just breathe."

He held my gaze and he must have seen something in my eyes because he nodded. "Justin," he began. "The last two and a half years have been a helluva road we've travelled. Some would call it hell, and some wouldn't have survived. But not us. We've come out better, stronger. Because steel has to go through fire to come out stronger." He let out a shaky breath. "Every day with you is a gift, and I promise to cherish you always. I will never take you for granted, not for a single second. I love you, Juss. Always have, always will. And I am proud to call you my husband."

I got a little teary and had to wave my hand in front of my face so the tears wouldn't fall. A few people laughed, and then it was Dallas who squeezed my hand.

God, now it was my turn . . .

I took a deep breath in and let it out slowly. "Dallas. You have been, without a doubt, a mountain of strength. Through everything, every procedure, every ordeal, you never took a backward step. And because of you, every step I've taken, no matter how small, has been forward. And I'm more in love with you than I thought was ever possible." I smiled at him. "After my accident, I spent a lot of time wishing for my memories to come back. I was missing pieces of my life, and pieces of myself were gone. But there was always you. And through it all, I realised the pieces of us were what kept me together." I squeezed his hands. "I promise you, Dallas, that I will love you forever. You are the reason I get up in the morning and the reason I try to be a better man than I was the day before. And I am proud and honoured and lucky as hell to call you my husband."

The celebrant smiled. "Dallas, do you take Justin to be your husband, to love always—"

"Yes," he blurted. "Yes, I do."

I laughed, and our guests laughed too. But then he slid my wedding ring over my finger and another piece of my heart slotted into place.

"Justin, do you take Dallas to be your husband—"

"Yes! I do."

The celebrant laughed, and I took Dallas' ring and gently put it on his finger. His smile, the tears in his eyes, stole the breath from my lungs.

"Okay then," the celebrant said. "I now pronounce you married. You may kiss your husband."

Dallas cupped my face and kissed me, not like we'd planned and not like we'd practised, but there was so much emotion in that kiss . . . his hands were trembling, and when he pulled back, his eyes were glassy.

I nodded, because I knew. I felt it in my heart, in my soul.

We were married. Legally, our very own little family. I was so happy, so full of love and hope, I just could have burst.

We were hugged and congratulated and hugged some more. We had a casual reception at the surf club, which was basically just lunch with our nearest and dearest. We didn't want anything super fancy. We just wanted it to be official.

And as I sat with Dallas by my side and listened as he talked and laughed with everyone, the weight of the ring on my wedding finger settled something deep inside me. I turned the silver band with my thumb, feeling the smooth glide against my skin. It felt so right. It was as though something lost was found. I couldn't explain it or why it made me feel so content.

"You okay, Juss?" Dallas asked.

I must have zoned out. Everyone was looking at me. "Yeah, I'm great. Just . . . happy, daydreaming."

Sparra shot me a look as though he'd been trying to get my attention. Shit. I leaned in and spoke in Dallas' ear. "Babe, can I have the keys to the ute. I want to get a pill."

He was immediately concerned. "Are you okay? Today's been a lot . . ."

"I'm fine, Dall. Honestly, never felt this good."

He studied my face for a second, as though he was looking for a tell or sign that I had a headache. Seeing none, he handed over the key and went back to the conversation. Sparra followed me out, and not a second later, Davo joined us.

I handed them keys. "Be quick, but be careful. Drive safe."

They grinned as they ran off and gave it a few minutes before I went back to the table. Carissa and Lauren smiled because they were in on our little plan, and I took my seat. Dallas put his arm around my shoulder as he laughed with Jimmy and Toni's husband, and he was none the wiser at their absence, and thankfully he never asked for his keys back.

But, about forty minutes later, it was time for us to go. Dallas paid the tab while I thanked everyone for sharing our special day with us, and I saw him looking around for Davo and Sparra. He'd noticed they were gone.

When he was done, he made his way to Lauren and Carissa, no doubt to ask them where the boys had gone, and I was beginning to think something had gone wrong. They were taking too long and Dallas was going to find out . . .

"Where's Davo and Sparra?" he asked Lauren and Carissa. "I thought they must have been at the bar. Or in the bathrooms? Did something happen?"

"No," Lauren said quickly. She tried to smile and her gaze darted to me, something Dallas didn't miss at all.

"Juss, what's going on?"

And just then, thank God, Dall's blue ute came around the corner. And not only that, but our bikes were loaded onto the back.

Dallas spun to me. "What? Justin? What the hell?"

"Surprise," I squeaked. God, was his reaction good or bad? "I booked our honeymoon."

"Our bikes?"

I nodded. I'd ridden a little over the last twelve months. I'd even driven the ute a few times, but I was ready to get back into it. Starting now. "Yeah. A week at the beach house in Hallidays Point. The one we stayed at years ago. It's all organised. The boys are taking care of the shop, and Toni's got everything sorted."

Dallas looked over at Toni, and she gave him a bright smile and a nod. Then he looked at Lauren and Carissa. "You all knew about this . . ."

*Oh God. This was going bad.* "I wanted to surprise you with something special, Dall. Somewhere that meant something to us. Because I remember that place. When we went there last time. And I wanted to ride with you again. We haven't really had a chance to do that. Not since the accident—"

He took two huge strides and collected me in his arms, lifting me off the ground and kissing me. "Are we really going riding?"

I nodded. "We have a week. No trails, but maybe an easy circuit. Small steps, right?"

Dallas hugged me, tucking me into his side as Davo and Sparra got out of the ute and threw the keys to him. "You're welcome," Davo said, wearing a shit-eating grin. "It was just the one bag by the door?"

"Yep," I answered. "Beauty of having just one wardrobe."

Sparra put his arm around Carissa but he smiled at me. "Oh, and Squish is fed. I'll check on him every day, I promise."

"He likes fishing shows on TV," I said.

"Jusso," Sparra said flatly. "I'll feed him; I'll even pat and cuddle him. But I ain't watching fishing shows with him."

I laughed and looked up at Dallas. "Husband?"

He put his forehead to mine. "Yes?"

"Are you ready to go?"

"We're leaving for our honeymoon right now?"

"Yep. Everything's taken care of."

We got into the ute, waving goodbye to our friends and family, and Dallas took my hand. I brought our joined hands to my lips and kissed the wedding ring on his finger. "Husband. I really like the sound of that."

"I really like you saying that," he said with a heated look in his eyes.

"Then we better get going. There's a certain sofa I remember in that beach house, and I remember what you did to me on it. I want to see if it's still there."

He laughed and started the engine. "I can't believe you planned this without me knowing."

I smiled as we began the drive north. I turned my wedding ring with my thumb and watched as the sun caught the gleam. "I can't wait."

"Can't wait for what?"

"Everything. Being married, beginning our lives as husbands, being happy forever."

Dallas grinned. "Me either, baby."

Exhaustion settled over me. A tiredness I hadn't felt in a while. I yawned and tried to shake it off. "Dunno why I'm so tired."

"Because you can finally relax," he offered with a smile. "After all the build-up and excitement of the wedding, it's over. Have a nap, baby." He gave me a wicked smile. "You're gonna need your energy later."

"Hmm, sounds promising." The truth was, I *was* tired, and a nap sounded pretty good. Especially if he intended to wear me out later . . .

I kept hold of his hand and closed my eyes and allowed the warmth through the windscreen and the hum of the tyres on the highway lull me to sleep.

———

A GENTLE HAND on my arm woke me. "Juss, baby, we're here."

I sat up straight and took in my surroundings. I was still in the ute, but we were stopped out the front of a familiar house.

Oh my God.

I got out and looked around. The trees, the sand, the smell . . . No one ever prepares you for the missing senses of memory loss. It's not just the memory itself, it's how it feels, how it smells and sounds, how it tastes.

But I remembered this place.

I turned to the house and followed Dallas up onto the front porch decking. He opened the glass sliding door and inside was a pale cream kitchen, a dining table, and a sofa . . .

"I remember this," I said. Dall smiled at me, but he didn't get it. "No, Dallas, I remember this. Everything. I remember us being here before, years ago. I remembered this all before, but seeing it . . ."

Dallas came back to the doorway and wrapped me up in his big, strong arms and held me tight. "Oh, baby."

"It's so weird. I remember you coming up from the beach, right there," I said, pointing toward the ocean. "You were wet and freezing cold, laughing. I remember riding our bikes from here. I remember us cooking noodles, and I remember cuddling up on the couch because we got back late and it was cold. I remember that couch . . . Dallas, I remember it."

Dallas pulled back a little so he could see my eyes. "I remember too."

The complete love and devotion he had for me was in his eyes, written on his face. "I meant what I said in our vows," I murmured. *God, was that just today?* "For a long time, there's been parts of me that felt incomplete. Maybe even before the accident. Then I woke up in hospital and the most amazing man was sitting there, already in love with me. Like I was the luckiest guy in the world. And it took a little while as I tried to put the puzzle of myself back together. But Dallas, it was the pieces of us that made me whole. Not me by myself, and not just you, but us."

He kissed me softly. "The pieces of us make me whole too."

Then he bent down and scooped me up, bridal style. "What are you doing?"

He grinned. "Carrying you across the threshold. It's not our house, but it is our wedding day."

I laughed as he stepped inside and put me gently on my feet next to the couch. "I love you, Dallas."

He beamed. "And I love you. Always have."

I sighed, content and safe in his love. "Always will."


The End

## ABOUT THE AUTHOR

N.R. Walker is an Australian author, who loves her genre of gay romance. She loves writing and spends far too much time doing it, but wouldn't have it any other way.

She is many things: a mother, a wife, a sister, a writer. She has pretty, pretty boys who live in her head, who don't let her sleep at night unless she gives them life with words.

She likes it when they do dirty, dirty things… but likes it even more when they fall in love.

She used to think having people in her head talking to her was weird, until one day she happened across other writers who told her it was normal.

She's been writing ever since…

## ALSO BY N.R. WALKER

*Blind Faith*

*Through These Eyes (Blind Faith #2)*

*Blindside: Mark's Story (Blind Faith #3)*

*Ten in the Bin*

*Gay Sex Club Stories 1*

*Gay Sex Club Stories 2*

*Point of No Return – Turning Point #1*

*Breaking Point – Turning Point #2*

*Starting Point – Turning Point #3*

*Element of Retrofit – Thomas Elkin Series #1*

*Clarity of Lines – Thomas Elkin Series #2*

*Sense of Place – Thomas Elkin Series #3*

*Taxes and TARDIS*

*Three's Company*

*Red Dirt Heart*

*Red Dirt Heart 2*

*Red Dirt Heart 3*

*Red Dirt Heart 4*

*Red Dirt Christmas*

*Cronin's Key*

*Cronin's Key II*

*Cronin's Key III*

*The Dichotomy of Angels*

*Throwing Hearts*

*Pieces of You - Missing Pieces #1*

*Pieces of Me - Missing Pieces #2*

*Pieces of Us - Missing Pieces #3*

Titles in Audio:

*Cronin's Key*

*Cronin's Key II*

*Cronin's Key III*

*Red Dirt Heart*

*Red Dirt Heart 2*

*Red Dirt Heart 3*

*Red Dirt Heart 4*

*The Weight Of It All*

*Switched*

*Point of No Return*

*Breaking Point*

*Starting Point*

*Spencer Cohen Book One*

*Spencer Cohen Book Two*

*Spencer Cohen Book Three*

*Yanni's Story*

*On Davis Row*

*Evolved*

Translated Titles:

*Fiducia Cieca* (Italian translation of *Blind Faith*)

*Attraverso Questi Occhi* (Italian translation of *Through These Eyes*)

*Preso alla Sprovvista* (Italian translation of *Blindside*)

*Il giorno del Mai* (Italian translation of *Blind Faith 3.5*)

*Cuore di Terra Rossa* (Italian translation of *Red Dirt Heart*)

*Cuore di Terra Rossa 2* (Italian translation of *Red Dirt Heart 2*)

*Cuore di Terra Rossa 3* (Italian translation of *Red Dirt Heart 3*)

*Cuore di Terra Rossa 4* (Italian translation of *Red Dirt Heart 4*)

*Natale di terra rossa* (*Red dirt Christmas*)

*Intervento di Retrofit* (Italian translation of *Elements of Retrofit*)

*A Chiare Linee* (Italian translation of *Clarity of Lines*)

*Senso D'appartenenza* (Italian translation of *Sense of Place*)

*Spencer Cohen 1 Serie: Spencer Cohen*

*Spencer Cohen 2 Serie: Spencer Cohen*

*Spencer Cohen 3 Serie: Spencer Cohen*

*Spencer Cohen 4 Serie: Yanni's Story*

*Punto di non Ritorno* (Italian translation of *Point of No Return*)

*Punto di Rottura* (Italian translation of *Breaking Point*)

*Punto di Partenza* (Italian translation of *Starting Point*)

*Imago* (Italian translation of *Imago*)

*Il desiderio di un soldato* (Italian translation of *A Soldier's Wish*)

*Confiance Aveugle* (French translation of *Blind Faith*)

*A travers ces yeux: Confiance Aveugle 2* (French translation of *Through These Eyes*)

*Aveugle: Confiance Aveugle 3* (French translation of *Blindside*)

*À Jamais* (French translation of *Blind Faith 3.5*)

*Cronin's Key* (French translation)

*Cronin's Key II* (French translation)

*Au Coeur de Sutton Station* (French translation of *Red Dirt Heart*)

*Partir ou rester* (French translation of *Red Dirt Heart 2*)

*Faire Face* (French translation of *Red Dirt Heart 3*)

*Trouver sa Place* (French translation of *Red Dirt Heart 4*)

*Le Poids de Sentiments* (French translation of *The Weight of It All*)

*Lodernde Erde* (German translation of *Red Dirt Heart*)

*Flammende Erde 2* (German translation of *Red Dirt Heart 2*)

*Vier Pfoten und ein bisschen Zufall* (German translation of *Finders Keepers*)

*Ein Kleines bisschen Versuchung* (German translation of *The Weight of It All*)

*Ein Kleines Bisschen Fur Immer* (German translation of *A Very Henry Christmas*)

*Weil Leibe uns immer Bliebt* (German translation of *Switched*)

*Drei Herzen eine Leibe* (German translation of *Three's Company*)

*Sixty Five Hours* (Thai translation)

*Finders Keepers* (Thai translation)

# AUTHOR NOTE

---

*"I lost a lot of pieces of my life. There are years still missing from my memory, but I have found so much more." I looked up at Dallas, seeing only love in his eyes. "The pieces of us are all that matter."*

---

To all my readers,
Thank you for loving Dallas and Justin as much as me. And thank you for taking this journey of recovery with them.